FORGOTTEN
SOULS

FORGOTTEN SOULS

ROOSTER SMITH

The Book Guild Ltd

First published in Great Britain in 2019 by
The Book Guild Ltd
9 Priory Business Park
Wistow Road, Kibworth
Leicestershire, LE8 0RX
Freephone: 0800 999 2982
www.bookguild.co.uk
Email: info@bookguild.co.uk
Twitter: @bookguild

Typeset in Garamond

Printed and bound in Great Britain by 4edge Limited

ISBN 978 1912575 671

British Library Cataloguing in Publication Data.
A catalogue record for this book is available from the British Library.

Printed on FSC accredited paper

This book is dedicated to anyone who reads it.
I wanted to shock and to scare, and I hope that I did a good job. This
is for you all...
Thank you.

Those souls asleep will return to reap…

THE DAWNING

A deathly screech was heard in the distance as an owl let out its cry in the night. An eerie mist began to roll across the field in this cold, evil place where the darkness seemed to creep up and enshroud you like death's blanket. A church bell rang thirteen times, then slowly, from out of the mist, the ghostly shapes of unholy children of differing ages started to form and with each passing second, they appeared more solid than before. They were all a sickly shade of grey with scruffy hair and rags for clothes. Every one of them had a stone-cold stare and a feeling of demonic evil all around them, and it was obvious that they were all wicked supernatural souls.

Walking behind these wretched urchins loomed the tall figure of a man. He was dressed in a black top hat, black trousers, and a long double-tailed coat. His polished shoes glistened as the moonlight struck them, and around the brim of his hat there was a purple silk band which had the King of Clubs playing card neatly slotted into it.

This sinister-looking man was also holding a silver-topped cane and his appearance seemed un-naturally out of time and he cared for the degenerates all around him like a father would to his own children. A thin, evil smile ran across his face as he watched more of his depraved offspring appear and it seemed that all was going to plan.

The field itself was nothing special and was just outside of the small seaside town of Mablethorpe. The field was inland from the sea, but it was still near enough to hear the waves breaking on the cold, windy beach. There were trees and bushes along two sides of the field and a small wire fence bordered the other edge separating it from the meadow next door. The field faced onto a narrow lane which was the main coastal road and it was the type of field you could have driven past many times without even noticing it. Apart from the ghostly people, the only other thing in the field was a circle of old, partly buried stones in the far corner. Were these to become more important in the future?

With an evil laugh, the tall man took off his top hat and revealed a shaved head. With the hat in one hand and his cane in the other, he held his arms out wide while standing behind his evil family and bellowed, "I, the Entertainer, now give you the life you were once denied. Go on, my children, go out and entertain!"

This pleased the young ones, and they all laughed and giggled as they ran off in different directions and faded away into the shadows of the night, departing the field to begin their mischief.

The evil-looking man who was obviously proud and protective of his offspring slowly walked back into the field towards the stone circle and vanished as a loud crash of thunder roared high above him and rain started to fall. The thunder woke up a woman, and quickly she sat up in her bed. She felt a chill in the air and the night seemed tenser than usual. She glanced at her clock; it was five past midnight.

The woman was Maggie Sykes, the local psychic who some of the town's teenagers thought was quite mad. For most of the year she lived in a chalet in Mablethorpe and this is where she was at present. It was the usual type of Chalet Park with a small store next to a chip shop and cafe, and there was also a tavern and play areas for the children.

Maggie was restless, so she got out of bed, put on her dressing gown and went into the kitchen to make a much-needed coffee. She then took her mug and opened the chalet door to savour the night air and drink her coffee in the moonlight. She had a feeling of impending doom and evil but she just couldn't put her finger on what the cause might be. Part of her hoped it was just a silly feeling, but she knew that this strange feeling was due to some impending peril.

Finishing her coffee, she put on her slippers and coat and went for a walk around the holiday park. She quietly walked between the caravans and chalets, not wanting to disturb their sleeping residents or scare the rabbits that were hopping about in the dark. After about three minutes she stopped and looked up into the eerie sky. The moon lit up a strange cloud, which looked like three small circular clouds formed into one with a stalk-like tail underneath it.

Maggie chuckled to herself. "That looks like a club."

She shivered in the breeze, so turned and walked back to her chalet. She quickly locked the door behind her and jumped back into her bed as the storm grew more intense.

APPREHENSION

The storm also woke up Louise, who was in the next town along the coast. She thought she heard a noise downstairs, so she tried to turn on the bedside lamp but nothing happened.

"Damn it – a power cut," she whispered to herself.

Not wanting to wake her husband, she slowly got out of bed, put on her dressing gown and reached for her cigarettes, lighter and mobile phone, intending to use the phone as a light as she goes downstairs.

As she walked down the stairs she began to make out the forms of her house. She couldn't see the stairs in front of her clearly, so she carefully felt for the next step by shuffling her feet. Suddenly, the form of a young child darted across the landing which made Louise shriek and stand rigid. After a few seconds she composed herself and shook her head – did she really see something or was it a trick of the dark?

She took a deep breath and continued her slow walk down the stairs as the ghostly face of a young girl appeared in the shadows behind her.

The banisters and walls flickered in the dull light and a sliver of moonlight escaped from under her son's bedroom door. In the gloom, a picture hanging on the wall looked like a man standing on the landing in front of her, and she reached out her hand to feel her way as she walked along. Her phone suddenly turned itself off, which made Louise jump in panic and she quickly turned it back on again. The house looked so different and evil in the blackness of the night.

Louise had the sense that she was being watched, but she knew that the rest of her family were all asleep and safe in their warm beds. After what seemed like a lifetime of walking through the gloom, she reached the bottom step and was in the hallway. She opened the cupboard in front of her and fumbled for the fuse box to check it. The fuses all seemed fine, so she went into the kitchen, raised the blind, and looked out of the window. No other lights were on in the street, including the lamp posts. Louise let out a long sigh as she realised that there was indeed a power cut – nothing to worry about. How wrong could she be?

Once more, her mobile turned itself off, but this time Louise couldn't turn it back on again.

"Bloody battery!" she exclaimed.

She opened a drawer and took out a candle, which she lit with the lighter from the pocket of her dressing gown. Turning slowly and shielding the flame with her hand, she started to walk back upstairs.

The flickering flame made the walk back up even more frightening than her walk down. All of the pictures seemed to come alive and dance on the walls, and every step was a cautious one. Halfway up the stairs she was startled by what sounded like a quiet but evil child's laugh. She spun around and looked down the stairs, which seemed like a long passageway disappearing into the darkness. There was nothing there. With another long sigh, she turned and continued her anxious journey back up to her bed, but didn't see the face of the ungodly brat slowly appear in a hanging picture she had walked past many times before.

After a few more nervous paces she reached the top step, and was just about to step up onto it when from out of nowhere the ghostly, evil girl appeared and pointed at Louise. With its deathly white finger raised in front of Louise's face, it uttered the word, "Mummy."

Before Louise could even scream, the child grabbed both of her shoulders and pushed her backwards and Louise fell down the stairs. She staggered to her feet, dazed on the landing halfway down, and then the girl appeared again and pushed her down the rest of the stairs. She went banging and rolling down the stairs to the horrible cracking and breaking of her bones, and then came to an abrupt and painful stop in the hallway.

She was covered in cuts and blood was coming out of her ears and nose. The frightened woman sat up, and the numbness from the fall quickly wore off. She cried out in pain when she saw that her leg was horribly twisted and obviously broken; her wrist was also twisted badly. She then realised what had just happened and that the child could still be there so she held her hand tightly over her mouth so no noise would come from her lips. In her panic she didn't even think about shouting out for her husband. The darkness seemed to close in on her as she painfully fumbled around for the candle and found it against the nearby wall. Slowly, and with another muffled cry of pain, she got her lighter from out of her pocket and lit the candle. The reflection of the flame danced and flickered on the walls as Louise slowly turned her head and looked around the hallway for the demonic creature. All seemed quiet, but she was breathing faster and faster in anticipation of what might happen next. Her fear was unbearable.

Suddenly the ghostly child appeared in front of Louise with an evil smile on her face. The child again pointed at Louise and again whispered, "Mummy."

Louise was more scared than she had ever been in her entire life, but she found her strength and replied, "I don't understand; I'm not your mother."

"No, you're not," the phantom moaned as she pointed her bony finger at her, "but you should've been."

Then with a strange supernatural power which all of the Entertainer's children had, the girl blew onto the flame of the candle which instantly became a raging fire that quickly engulfed Louise. The frightful screams of her agony rang throughout the house as the fire quickly covered her and burnt away her hair. There was the awful stench of cooking flesh as the heat blistered her soft white skin, which peeled off and melted away and fell to the carpet as she slowly burnt to death, fused onto the hallway floor by the fierce heat. Her skinless, bony hands tried to extinguish the flames and her white teeth could be seen flashing in the fire as her lips dissolved in the inferno.

Her husband, hearing the commotion, came running down the stairs, but the heat was too great and he couldn't reach his wife as the fire raged more violently but somehow the inferno was centred on Louise and didn't spread too much from her.

"Louise!" he screamed.

And as he looked on helplessly at the truly gruesome sight before his pained eyes, in a strained, weak voice Louise groaned, "Child."

Her head fell lifelessly onto her shoulder as her husband tried frantically to put out the flames with his bare and bleeding hands. As his palms danced around in the fire, he didn't notice the King of Clubs playing card which was immune to the flames float down by his wife's side and more disturbing was that he didn't see the ghostly child fade away either.

***

Steve Carlton, the town's main detective, was asleep in his bed when he was suddenly woken up by the ringing of the telephone. Stretching out his hand and without looking, he reached for the phone and held it to his ear while still deep under the blankets.

"Hello," he muttered with a dry mouth. "What's wrong?"

He knew that there must be some kind of trouble as he was used to late-night police calls.

Steve suddenly sat bolt upright, and with a serious look on his face said, "I'm on my way." It was clear to him from the call that something terrible had happened.

About half an hour later he arrived at the gruesome scene at Louise's house. He walked up the path to the front door, and from out of the house a young policewoman burst past him and was sick on the grass. Steve took a deep breath.

"Damn, it must be a good 'un," he whispered.

He walked into the house to a hive of activity. Police photographers were busy clicking their cameras all around the hallway and stairs and the forensic team were walking about in their white overalls. Steve walked up to a forensic officer.

"What's happened, Gary?"

Gary, who loved gruesome and ghastly crime scenes, smiled and led Steve the few short steps to where Louise was sitting on the floor. With an out-of-place happy grin he said to his boss, "That's what happened."

Steve looked down at the burnt body fused to the carpet by the vicious heat it had been subjected to earlier, and his eyes widened with shock.

"My God, the heat must have been horrendous."

"It was," Gary commented, "but it didn't burn the carpet or the walls, so it's a strange one."

Steve turned and looked into the kitchen where he saw a man who was obviously the heartbroken husband sitting on a chair, sobbing. He beckoned a policewoman from out of the kitchen and questioned her.

"Has he said what happened yet?"

The policewoman nodded and replied, "Yes, he's Jon Bond, the husband, and he said he was woken by screams and there was a power cut. He ran down the stairs and saw Louise already on fire and there was nothing he could do but watch her burn to death."

Steve glanced at Jon and then back to the officer. "Could he have done this himself?"

She shook her head. "I don't think so he's devastated and his hands are all burnt up because he tried to put out the fire. There is something else though."

Steve knew that a strange revelation was about to come his way as he sighed, "OK, what is it?"

"Well, Jon said that she muttered the word 'child' as she burned," the woman proclaimed. "It's an odd thing to say for your last word, isn't it?"

Steve agreed. "Yes, but she could have meant for Jon to look after their child because she knew she was doomed? People can say odd things when faced with death."

The policewoman shook her head. "They have two children, sir, not one."

They looked at each other, both sensing that there was something more sinister about all of this.

Gary called Steve over to the charred body. "Here, Steve, take a look at this."

Steve knelt down beside Gary and saw the King of Clubs playing card on the carpet. Gary took a pair of tweezers out of his jacket pocket and carefully picked up the card. He turned it round and looked at the back, and saw a picture of a silver-topped cane running diagonally from top left to bottom right. On the top right-hand side above the angled cane was a top hat with a purple ribbon around its brim.

Steve and Gary stared at each other as they both realised that this was some kind of calling card left by the murderer, and in cases like this there were usually more to come.

Steve got back onto his feet. "Keep me up to date with things, Gary; I'll see you in the morning. There's nothing I can do here but question the husband as this card didn't burn in the fire and I want to know why."

He left the house, got into his car, and drove away with his mind racing, thinking about what might be coming next.

ROLLER

Later that morning in Mablethorpe, Josh Adamson, an author of the strange and supernatural, woke up to the sun shining through his bedroom window. He could hear his wife Rosie downstairs in the kitchen, clattering the cups together as she made a morning coffee. Josh rubbed his eyes, yawned, and went downstairs. As he reached the bottom of the staircase Rosie came out of the kitchen holding two cups of coffee.

She smiled. "Morning, dear," she said as she kissed Josh on his cheek.

She then went straight into the living room before Josh could kiss her back. He followed and kissed Rosie as she sat on the sofa. There were some rounds of toast on a plate on the coffee table, and Rosie was scoffing them down as she had to get to work. She was a teacher at the local primary school and she was running a bit late that morning.

Josh smiled at her, and with a chuckle said, "Slow down, dear; you'll be on time."

"It's all right for some," she replied, putting her now-empty cup down onto the table. "Not all of us have the luxury of working from home."

Rosie got up and went into the hallway to put her coat on. Josh followed, and Rosie turned to him.

"I'll cook us that bacon for our tea later," she said, slinging on her coat. "What are you doing today?"

Josh exhaled heavily. "I'm going to try and get some inspiration to finish my book, but I'll do the housework first."

They kissed again.

"See you later, then," Rosie chuckled. "I know you like wearing my apron."

She ran out of the door, closing it behind her and leaving a laughing Josh standing alone in the hall.

***

It was now about 8.40am and the sun was shining through some thin morning clouds, and all of the towns and villages along the stretch of coast where Josh lived were getting ready for the day. Shops and cafes were opening and market stalls were having their covers ripped off ready for the day's trading to begin.

George, who had lived in Ingoldmells all of his adult life and who was well known to the other locals, was walking to work, but as he was in a hurry, he didn't notice an ashen-looking child following him.

George suddenly became uneasy and spun around as he felt that he was being watched, but found that he was all alone in the street. It was quite a long street lined with a few trees and not a lot of houses, and the houses that were scattered throughout the area were older and some of them were being demolished to make space for new builds. He then heard an infant's cry ring out. The painful wail seemed to echo and fill the area but it didn't seem to have any fixed point as to where it came from, which confused George.

He looked all around but couldn't see a child, so, feeling a little scared, called out, "Hello, is anybody there?"

The cry stopped as abruptly as it started, and all was silent once again.

George continued his walk down the street, but with each stride he looked around. He crossed a road and walked towards some building work outside an old abandoned house. Most of what remained of the house was its brick shell, the kind of house you used to play in as a child. Its windows were gone and the entire upper level had been demolished. Through the gaps in the walls where the windows and doors once stood, you could see the piles of stone and rubble left by the builders. George passed a small digger and a mini road roller as some groundwork was also going on, and as he reached the house he looked through one of the window gaps and was startled when a small boy jumped up onto the window ledge. This young, scruffy, degenerate lad was crying, so George felt he had to do something.

"Hello, I thought I heard your cry earlier," he said in a calm manner so he didn't further upset the boy. "Are you all right?"

The boy smiled and muttered, "You're my daddy."

"No, I'm not," George stated with a grin, "but let's get you out of there as it's not safe."

He reached up to the boy to help him down from the ledge, but the urchin leant against the unsafe wall, which sent it crashing down onto a shrieking George.

Trapped on his back underneath the pile of mortar and rubble, George was pinned down, unable to move. All that was sticking out from under the mound was his head, but he was still conscious. He felt the weight crushing his ribs and legs and squeezing the air from his lungs. Coughing and spluttering, George slowly turned his head and assessed his dilemma. George still had some air left in his slowly compressing lungs and he let out a cry of pain as his neck cracked, sending a sharp pain all through his mangled body, so he stopped moving.

"Boy, where are you?" he managed to utter in agony. "Help me."

George was relieved when the small boy appeared, standing above him.

"Thank God – go and get help."

The infant walked away and George felt a bit better knowing that help would soon arrive. He managed another weak breath to get some much-needed air into his lungs, but his new-found hope was soon to be dashed.

George heard the sound of the nearby road roller he had previously walked past start up. The sound grew louder and louder, and George became scared.

"Hello, who's there?" he wailed, but no reply came his way. The vehicle slowly drew nearer and nearer, so George painfully turned his head to face it and was horrified at what he saw.

The devil child was sitting in the roller and, with evil black eyes which looked like wells in the snow against his pale skin, was staring directly at the prone man trapped under the heavy blanket of bricks. The roller was a slow-moving machine and George could see every dent and piece of dirt and sand on the powerful, heavy wheel being driven towards him.

"No, stop!" he yelled as loud as he could. "Find the brake!"

But it was to no avail; the boy was not going to stop his deadly mission and he seemed to take pleasure in knowing what was to come, and there was nothing at all that George could do as he was helpless to stop the approach.

The roller drew nearer to George and he could now feel the ground under his head rumble and vibrate. His eyes shook in their sockets but all he could do was watch in terror as the heavy-duty machine was almost upon him. The iron wheel turned and moved closer and closer, and George's eyes opened wide. He knew he was doomed.

With a last cry of fear he yelled, "No, please stop!", but the child continued to drive the machine. George turned his face away from the roller and was just about to give out his last scream, but it was too late as the roller finally reached his head and slowly began to roll over it. The heavy front wheel was relentless as it hit George's skull contorting its features.

With a sickening loud crack, George's fate was sealed. The roller crushed his head and his eyes popped out and shot along the pavement in a spurt of blood which also splattered the iron wheel. His skull slowly smashed and came apart, and George's brain was soon exposed with each falling away of bone. As the vehicle rolled over his head it suddenly exploded in a hail of blood, brain, hair and bone which covered the wheel and the surrounding pavement in a messy puddle of filth.

The evil boy continued to drive the roller until it had cleared where George had lain, but where his head once was there was now only a massive, disgusting bloodstain with small pieces of bone and tissue mixed in, and George's lifeless eyes were staring up into the sky from the ground nearby. The urchin got down from the roller and placed a King of Clubs card in the pool of blood and bone, then he walked down the road and faded away, leaving the scene of chaos in his wake ready to be discovered by the builders when they turned up for work.

AT THE BANK

A few days later, Maggie Sykes was reading of the two strange deaths when she shivered and suddenly became aware that they may somehow be connected. She put down the newspaper and left her chalet.

Maggie got into her car, but just before she drove away the image of a man wearing a top hat flashed in her rear-view mirror. She screamed, then, composing herself she summoned the nerve to look into the mirror again, but all she saw was her own reflection. Anyone else would have just been relieved, but as Maggie was psychic she knew that it must have meant something more. She drove into town and locked her car to start her walk to the bank.

***

Alan, a local shopkeeper, was also walking through the town when he had the uneasy feeling that he was being followed. He spun around and glimpsed the figure of a dishevelled young boy. A passer-by blocked his view for a split second, and when his view cleared the boy was gone. Did he really see him?

Alan continued his journey, but became more scared with each step he took. He felt terrified but didn't know why.

He crossed a road, and directly in front of him was the dirty, dishevelled lad once again. The child just glared at Alan and let out a loud, piercing scream, and as he did so, his mouth became unnaturally wide, his jaw dropping so much that it hit his chest, revealing a large black hole where his mouth should be. Alan stared in horror, but all of the other people in the area seemed to be oblivious to this malevolent presence.

Alan looked around and couldn't believe the passing crowds were ignoring this unholy, impish child. He blinked, and the boy was gone. With his fear now growing even more Alan walked a little faster towards the bank, but again he caught a glimpse of the youngster in the crowd. Breathing shallower and a lot quicker, he tried to ignore his vision as he broke out into a trot. As he passed a shop window he saw the evil boy inside with his mouth again open wide in a silent scream, and the mite didn't take his eyes off Alan, who quickened his stride. Alan was now in a blind panic and he burst into the bank, violently pushing open the doors in front of him.

The people already inside all turned and glared at him due to his rude and noisy entry, and the room suddenly fell quiet. Alan felt embarrassed but also relieved, as he was no longer alone but surrounded by the other customers who were talking and waiting in line. He looked around the room to see if his fiendish follower was there, but there was no sign of the ghostly child. The bank's customers all turned away to attend to their business, and Alan joined a queue. Maggie Sykes then entered the building and joined a different line.

At last Alan reached the counter and was just about to get out his bank card when he suddenly became filled with fear once more. He looked behind the cashier and saw the demonic young boy standing against the wall behind her, pointing straight at him.

"Look!" Alan shouted at Rachel, the cashier, as he pointed at the child. "There, you must see him!"

Rachel turned around in her chair and looked at the wall, but she saw nothing.

"Sorry, sir, I don't know what you mean."

Alan's eyes widened and his heart raced, and again he pointed at the evil boy. This time he yelled at the top of his voice, "There, look at him!"

Rachel quickly glanced backwards, but again she saw nothing.

"Please calm down, sir, or I'll have to call security," she said, sensing a situation developing.

Alan turned to the other people in the room. "Look, someone must see him!" he shouted once more, but everyone thought he must be mad and ignored him. Even Maggie couldn't see the urchin standing behind the cashier; however she could sense something was amiss and she had a feeling of foreboding.

Alan turned back and again pointed towards the evil boy, but this time he leant over the counter a bit further, and as he did so he brushed against Rachel making her knee hit a button underneath the counter. This activated a tough Perspex security screen which suddenly shot straight up from the counter towards the ceiling, and as Alan was leaning over the counter, the screen hit him in his stomach and sent him upwards, pinning him to the ceiling with his legs on one side of the Perspex and his torso on the other side of it.

Everyone in the bank yelled and screamed in fear for Alan, who was struggling for breath. He had blood spurting from his stomach which dripped down both sides of the plastic screen, and there was some trickling from his mouth as well. Some of his intestines began to seep out of the wound, and a muffled yelp came from his lips as he gasped for air. Rachel and another colleague held their hands up to Alan and tried to support him but they could barely stretch up high enough to help, and there were screams of panic coming from all around the room. Alan was violently grabbing at the plastic screen, but there was nothing to hold on to so his hands just slipped around on it, spreading his blood and making the screen even more slimy and messy.

On the other side of the Perspex, some of the customers were reaching up trying to help support Alan's kicking legs, and there was chaos all around the room. Alan was being crushed against the ceiling by the security screen and there was nothing that anyone could do.

They all watched in horror as a colleague shouted to Rachel, "Quick, press the release button!"

Rachel reached under the counter and pressed the

button, but the button just sparked, which made Rachel jump backwards and land on the floor in a heap. The screen didn't move. Rachel realised that Alan was doomed. With a sickening crack of bone, he let out a scream as blood poured from his wide-open mouth. His innards started to ooze out from the opening along his waist and his intestines began to slip down both sides of the plastic screen. Then suddenly, the screen violently shot up the last few inches and slammed into the ceiling. Alan was sliced completely in half.

Screams rang out all around the room as Alan's legs slowly slid down the screen, leaving a sickly trail as they hit the counter, and landed on the floor in a standing position with blood still spurting upwards from out of them, which splattered some of the customers. Entrails were flopping down from the hole in Alan's torso and although he was dead, his eyes were still wide open as his upper half slipped down the Perspex. There was an ear-piercing, high-pitched screech as his blood-soaked hands slid down the plastic and a river of blood and guts followed, leaving a long, slimy trail in its path.

Alan's torso fell away from the security screen and landed on the screaming Rachel, who suddenly found that she was staring directly into the dead man's contorted and pained face. With a loud scream she threw Alan's torso from her lap and it hit the wall with a ghastly splat.

As the panic continued throughout the room, a King of Clubs playing card materialised on the body of the dead man.

Maggie saw the playing card appear and thought she

saw a child from out of the corner of her eye but when she turned her head, no child was anywhere to be seen. A feeling of terror fell over her like a shroud, but she still didn't know what it all meant. She ran out of the bank and along the road, other people in the street were moving out of her way as she dashed along, heading for the police station. She burst in through the doors and ran straight up to the desk, where a surprised constable stared at her.

"Please, madam, calm down," he said to the obviously disturbed woman. "How can I help?"

Maggie composed herself. "There's been a horrible death at the bank."

The constable was stunned as Maggie continued, "It's all connected."

"Connected – what do you mean, connected?" the young officer asked.

"It has something to do with the other two weird deaths that happened this week, I just know it has."

The police officer started to write down what Maggie had just related to him.

"Now then, madam, tell me just how this is all connected."

Maggie's face dropped as she knew what was about to happen. "I can sense things," she informed the constable. "I know things that normal people can't understand."

The officer glared at the strange woman standing in front of him. "Hold on, madam, what's your name?"

A sigh came from her lips as she replied quietly, "Maggie Sykes."

The officer tore the page from his notebook and threw

it into the waste bin. "Maggie Sykes… ah yes, you have wasted our time many times before, haven't you? Go on, get out."

He pointed to the door, and as Maggie had been in this situation before she knew it was not worth wasting her breath, so she turned and left the station, knowing that she wouldn't be believed.

QUARTERED

About two weeks later, Alan's funeral was taking place at the local cemetery. It was a small cemetery with lots of green, moss-covered headstones dotted all around. Some small, tomb-like memorials broke up the lines of headstones and there was the beautiful aroma of fresh flowers all around the well-kept graveyard. All of Alan's family were there, but they didn't notice that Maggie was also watching the proceedings.

She knew something was going on in the town and the surrounding area and thought she might see or sense something at the funeral, especially as she had witnessed Alan's demise.

Maggie noticed a blonde woman weeping near the graveside and she had the feeling that this woman was important to the events. Then she had a stroke of luck. All of the family went over to the chapel to thank the vicar, but the blonde woman decided to walk around the graveyard. Maggie saw her chance and walked along the adjoining paths through the gravestones and slowly met up with the woman.

"Hello dear." Maggie smiled at the woman. "It's a lovely day, but such a sad occasion."

The woman smiled back. "Yes, it is."

Maggie sensed the woman was about to weep, so she decided to break the potential awkwardness.

"I'm Maggie," she said softly, holding out her hand, hoping the grieving woman would shake it. "Did you know the deceased?"

"Michelle, and yes, I did know him," the woman answered while shaking Maggie's outstretched palm. "I used to go out with him when we were teenagers. We fell out, as you do, but we've remained friends for the last twenty years."

"Aw, that's a nice story," Maggie replied with a sad smile as their hands parted. She thought that this old connection could be of great importance.

"Anyway, I'd better be getting back," Michelle uttered as she glanced towards the chapel. "It's been nice talking to you."

She walked slowly back to the other mourners and Maggie left the cemetery to go home.

***

Michelle returned home after the funeral and decided to take a shower. When she looked into her bathroom mirror, she let out a gasp of horror as she saw a dishevelled young boy staring back at her. Unknown to her it was the same ghostly child that had previously killed Alan, her ex-boyfriend, at the bank.

Michelle blinked and looked into the mirror again, but the boy had vanished. Did she imagine it?

Thinking that it was just her mind playing tricks on her after the stressful day she had just had, she turned on the shower. With the water flowing from the shower head, she returned to the mirror and began to wash away her make-up.

Suddenly the ghastly reflection of the devilish boy reappeared behind her, and Michelle let out a loud, frightened scream. The evil mite then grabbed Michelle's head and smashed her face into the mirror with such force that she was knocked unconscious and splinters of glass pierced her skin.

After a while, Michelle slowly regained consciousness and came to her senses. She quickly realised that she was in a field and her hands and feet were tied to four snorting horses. She started to struggle and thrash about to try to break free, but her bonds were too tight and her struggle was in vain. She turned her head to see if anyone else was around.

"Hello is there somebody there?" she hollered, but no reply came. Now in a panic, she shouted at the top of her voice, "Help me! Can anybody hear me? Please help me!"

She heard the grass rustle under someone's footsteps, and suddenly became more frightened and racked with greater fear and dread.

"Who's there?" she muttered, as she was now too scared to shout.

A gust of deathly wind blew across her, making her blink, and when she opened her eyes again she saw the same strange young boy she had seen in her bathroom mirror standing above her.

"Who are you?" she asked.

The boy didn't move or answer her.

"What do you want with me?"

The four heaving horses grew impatient and restless, and the ropes that tied Michelle became tighter, pulling and lifting the bound victim a bit higher off the ground. She screamed in pain as she felt her limbs stretching and slowly being pulled from their joints. There was an awful crack of bone as Michelle's knee was ripped apart, but it still remained attached to her leg by the slenderest of sinews.

Blood and tissue began to pour from this wound, and it splashed down onto the grass, turning it from the lush shade of green it once was into an awful puddle of dirty scarlet. A few seconds later, her shoulder snapped and became dislocated and contorted, which forced a thin shard of bone to shoot out through her skin. Blood and body fluid began to pump from the gash, and Michelle screamed in agony.

"No! Please stop, let me go!" she begged, but it was to no avail.

With the horses pulling harder and harder and Michelle's body being stretched to bursting point, she knew her torture was nearly at an end. With one last desperate glance towards the evil urchin, and sensing her impending death, she held what was to be her last breath.

All around her became strangely silent and still, but then the vile nestling opened his mouth, just as he had before with Alan. It became so wide that once again it filled his face and his chin dropped onto his chest. With an unnaturally strong breath, the child let out a high-pitched shriek which pierced the air. This scared the horses, which made them all pull away and run off.

The ropes were strong, and as the beasts galloped off into the field in their different directions, the bones in Michelle's limbs fractured and snapped and her legs and arms were finally ripped away from her helpless body, which was then flung high up into the air. The limbs spurted out their bloody contents as they were carried off, still tied to the horses, and as they were dragged through the grass they left a sickly crimson trail. Michelle's lifeless body came back down onto the grass with a horrible thud and her bloodshot eyes stared blankly up into the sky.

The loathsome boy knelt down beside what was left of the woman, and a tall man wearing a top hat walked up and stood behind him.

"Well done, my child," he whispered to the boy as he took a King of Clubs card from the silk band around his hat and handed it to the boy, who put it on the bloodied torso. Magically, there still remained a King of Clubs card in the hatband – a sleight-of-hand magic trick or something else?

The man helped the boy to his feet. "Come on, let's go." He beamed at the child. "For now, your work is done."

BLISTER

Maggie was reading the morning paper when her face suddenly became a horrible shade of grey. She read the story of Michelle's death in the field, and this confirmed to her that the strange deaths were connected. She remembered that Michelle told her that she used to date Alan years ago, so again she went to the police station. This time, the police listened to her.

Steve Carlton interviewed Maggie, and he asked how she knew the deaths were connected.

"I came in a few days ago and tried to tell your constable, but now I have proper evidence," Maggie began. "Alan and Michelle used to be boyfriend and girlfriend when they were teenagers, and if you investigate deeper you may find that the other victims were also somehow connected – that Louise woman and George."

"OK, I think you may have something here," Steve replied with a nod. "I'll check out what you've told me." He already knew that the deaths were connected due to the King of Clubs calling card left behind at every scene.

There was a knock at the door, and Josh Adamson popped his head around and peered into the room.

"Oh, sorry, Steve, I thought you were alone."

Steve rose from his chair. "Josh, come in; I've got someone I'd like you to meet."

Josh entered the room and Steve did the introductions.

"Josh, this is Maggie Sykes. Maggie, Josh Adamson."

Maggie and Josh shook hands, and as they did so, Maggie felt a strange sensation but she didn't say anything.

Steve continued, "Josh helps us when there are strange things going on; he's a writer of the supernatural and a very clever man."

This appealed to Maggie. "Really – the supernatural, eh?" she nodded as she said "I think we'll get along just fine together."

They all sat down at the table to discuss matters further, and Maggie was a bit happier now that she was being taken more seriously.

***

Cumberworth was a village, about two miles inland from the North Sea that had some quaint cottages in it. Most of these cottages had lush front gardens full of colourful blooms of all kinds and well-mowed lawns.

In one of the houses in this sleepy village, Tony, a builder, was going to have a bath. He had already turned on the taps and the bath was slowly filling up. Steam was slowly forming from the hot water, and Tony opened the cabinet on the wall to get out the shampoo. As he shut the cabinet door, he stepped back and fell over something. This made him spin around and grab at the shower curtain above the bath.

Still fully clothed, he tumbled backwards into the half-filled bath of hot water, and as he fell and splashed his head somehow became impaled on the tops of both bath taps.

Tony was stunned, looking straight up at the ceiling. The wall above the bath was wet from the splashes of bathwater. He came to his senses and let out an agonised scream as he felt the taps deeply embedded in the back of his head. Reaching behind him to assess the damage, Tony felt the back of his skull and a blind panic overcame his entire body.

"No!" he screamed as he felt the blood flowing from the holes in his head and the razor-sharp pieces of bone hanging from his smashed skull.

Tony tried to raise his head up from off the taps, but he only moved an inch before crying out in pain once more. He was stuck fast, and he could feel the soft tissue of his brain slowly spilling out from the gash in his head. He began to scream and thrash about in the rising hot water, and blood was now seeping from his ears and eyes. Moving was just too painful and dangerous, so Tony lay still and started to look around the bathroom in terror, not knowing what to do. Every breath he took was a short, sharp one.

He then heard a sound from the side of the bath, and slowly and painfully turned his head slightly to see what it was. He was horrified to see a young girl just standing there with an evil grin on her lips. She was about eleven years old and pale grey in colour, with scruffy brown hair and rags for clothes.

Without even wanting to know who she was or where she had come from, Tony muttered, "Help me."

The black-hearted wretch of a child put her cold hand onto his brow and pressed his head further down onto the taps, making the helpless man yell out with an agonised squeal as his skull was pushed down harder onto the metal taps piercing the delicate tissue of his exposed brain even more. She had the supernatural power to prolong a person's agony which all of the Entertainer's children seemed to have. The girl then took her hand away and Tony could breathe again. While the evil brat looked around the bathroom, Tony tried to break free from the taps. He fumbled around behind his head and screamed as he pulled away a piece of his skull. He dropped the fragment of bone into the bath and felt for the taps once more, and let out a blood-curdling yell as the sharp jagged edge of the gaping hole sliced off three of his fingers. The digits dropped into the bathwater and blood spurted from the stumps of his knuckles.

Tony looked up, and again he saw the malicious young girl. She was laughing at him, tightly gripping a toothbrush by the bristle end, and she had an evil glint in her eye. Tony was rigid with fright. He had the cold metal of the taps still embedded in his skull and blood gushing from the open wound. The water was rising and getting hotter, and his fear was growing with every second. All he could do was to watch in horror as the ghastly child raised her hand up high and then plunged the handle of the toothbrush into his eye.

The eyeball popped and blood jetted up into the air as Tony tried to scream, but no sound came from his mouth; he was in too much pain. The girl twisted the toothbrush round and round, and with a sickening rip, she pulled Tony's eye away from his head.

The veins and tendons stretched away from the socket and snapped off from the eyeball, which was still stuck to the end of the toothbrush. Tony slowly raised his blood-soaked hands to his face and began to tremble all over. He knew he was finished, but his agony wasn't over yet. The sinister mite threw Tony's eye to the floor and held out her hands towards him. Both of her hands seemed to glow and get hotter, and with a last evil grin, she plunged them into the bathwater.

The water began to get very hot very fast due to the girl's uncanny power and Tony cried out in agony as he was boiled alive. His skin began to blister and fall away into the water, turning it into porridge-like mush as it bubbled and boiled and the room filled with steam, giving off the horrible stench of cooking flesh and burning skin.

The girl then violently pulled her hands out from the bath, splashing water all over the room, and just stood there watching. She smiled and seemed to get pleasure from Tony's plight as he let out his parting groans. Suddenly the water boiled and flames burst out it was like the very fires of Hell shooting up through the bathwater and Tony was burnt to death in a stew of his own body fluids and blood.

The evil urchin let out a disappointed sigh as the flames suddenly died, leaving the charred body of her victim floating in the dirty, bloody water. She was sorry that she couldn't torture Tony and inflict even more agony and pain and that her mission was now complete. She gently placed the usual King of Clubs card down next to Tony's disembodied eye and faded away, leaving the gruesome eye staring at the playing card in the steam-filled room.

A moment later there was a knock on the bathroom door.

"Tony, are you OK?"

It was his wife; she had heard some splashing from downstairs and was curious to what Tony was doing. She became worried when he didn't reply.

She opened the door and let out a terrified scream as she saw the horror left behind by the evil child.

***

About an hour later, Tony's house and bathroom were a mass of activity with the police and forensic team examining the crime scene for evidence. Steve walked up the stairs and was again met by Gary, who took pleasure in immediately telling him of another gruesome demise.

"It's another good one, guv," Gary stated. "Impaled, scalded, and eye gouged out."

Steve wiped his worried brow with his hand. "King of Clubs?" he asked.

Gary nodded. "Yes, mate; no doubt it's the same person or persons as before."

"Damn it," Steve replied with a frown on his face. "The last thing we need is a nutter running around during the holiday season."

He walked over to the bath and saw what remained of Tony. There were still pieces of dead skin flaking off and floating about in the bath.

"The place is heaving with holidaymakers – that makes more potential victims than ever."

He left the house knowing that this was a lot more serious than he first thought.

DEADLY PILLOW

A car was travelling down a country lane with the driver's window wound down. Music was blasting from the vehicle and Sarah, the driver, was humming the tune and tapping her hand on the steering wheel to the beat of the song. The sun was shining and it flickered through the trees as she drove along. It was obvious that Sarah was having a good day, as she had a broad grin on her face and didn't seem to have a care in the world.

Still tapping the wheel, she suddenly shuddered all over and became a little colder. At that moment she glanced out of the open window and saw a tall man standing at the side of the road. She thought him strange as he was wearing a top hat and holding a cane and wouldn't look out of place in a horror movie. By his side was a teenage child, a scruffy-looking boy who had a mischievous smile on his thin, pale lips. As Sarah drove on she looked into the rear-view mirror and saw the child point at her and the sinister man nod in agreement.

"Weird," Sarah mumbled to herself.

She shrugged her shoulders and continued on with her journey still humming and tapping the steering wheel, enjoying the heat of the sun. Sarah then jumped a little as the CD started to jump and play the same words over and over again. Sarah reached towards the CD player and tried to eject the disc.

"That's all I need," she said, pressing the button.

The disc didn't eject, and the CD was still stuck on repeating the same words again and again. Sarah started to press the button a bit harder and faster.

"Come on, bloody come out," she groaned, and as she did so, she was distracted from her driving and started to swerve. Quickly grabbing the steering wheel with both hands again and actually looking at the road, she straightened the car up and drove on.

She was approaching her turn, so she flicked on the indicator to turn left and again pressed the button to try to eject the disc. With her hand still in front of the CD player, she glanced upwards and saw the scruffy young boy from earlier standing in the road. Sarah screamed and slammed on the brakes, but felt the sickening bump as she ploughed into the helpless child and drove over his body. As soon as she braked, the disc shot out from the CD player and lodged deep into her arm sending blood seeping from the wound. Her chest hit the steering wheel which caused her head to jolt forwards and she banged her forehead hard on the windscreen and was stunned as the car came to a stop. She looked at her arm and saw that the disc was deeply embedded in her arm just above the wrist and blood was spitting out and dripping down over her hand as the flow was still partially restricted by the disc, the blood then began to fall like deep red rain onto the gearstick. She pulled the disc from her arm and let out an agonised yell as the blood gushed out faster. Sarah then grabbed a cloth from the glovebox and held it to her wrist to stem the flow. Then, for some strange reason she forgot her own predicament and remembered the pale child she had just run over.

"Oh my God, the boy!" she cried, and she opened the door and painfully climbed out to see what devastation she had caused.

Sarah slowly and painfully walked around to the front of her car to see what was left of the child, but to her amazement there was no blood on the car and no sign of the boy. She gulped.

"Oh no, he's under the car."

She carefully knelt down and slowly bent as low as she could to look underneath the vehicle. Her eyes widened with shock as again there was no sign of the youth.

The puzzled woman then said to herself, "But I hit him, I ran over him."

Sarah stood up and winced in pain as she held her arm. She looked around the area and shouted, "Hello, are you there?" But all was silent.

She walked over to a grass verge and looked for the boy just to make sure he didn't bounce off the car, but nothing unusual was there; it was like he had totally vanished.

Sarah returned to her car and sat down. She adjusted the cloth on her arm, pulled an elastic band from her hair, and twisted it around the cloth to hold it in place. This made Sarah feel a bit more comfortable as the cloth seemed to stem the flow of blood, but she was still puzzled at what had just happened to her. She shook her head, regained her composure and started the car, but before she could drive away, the devilish boy suddenly appeared at the side of the vehicle. This made Sarah yell in surprise at his sudden reappearance, but she was relieved to actually see him.

"You scared me," she said to the dishevelled adolescent. "Are you all right?"

The boy walked up to the car and stood alongside the open window, but he said nothing, he just stood there glaring directly into her eyes. Sarah felt uncomfortable and thought she had to do something.

"Do you need me to take you home?" she asked, but the damned youngster didn't move or talk.

Sarah was getting scared now, and she didn't feel safe anymore as she began to sense something weird was happening.

"Look, I'm sorry I hit you but you just stepped out in front of me, didn't you?" She trembled as she tried to shift the blame onto the urchin.

The boy then put both of his pale hands onto the car door and leant in through the window. He was so close that Sarah could see the thin, black veins under his ghostly white skin, and there was a smell of death all around. The evil brat then opened his eyes as wide as he could, and Sarah couldn't bear the situation any longer.

"Look, it was your fault; you should've been looking where you were going. Get off the car and just go home!"

she yelled, and moved her finger towards the button to close the window.

This angered the child, and he violently banged on the steering wheel, which sent the airbag flying out. Sarah screamed as the large white pillow formed in front of her and tried to push it down, which made her yelp in pain from her injured arm.

"Now look at what you've done!" she shouted. "Go on; just get out of here before I do something I'll regret!"

There was an uneasy silence, but then the boy suddenly grabbed Sarah's head and pushed it into the inflated airbag, holding her down with uncanny strength.

Sarah's face was embedded in the pillow of air, and her arms flailed about as she tried to grab the child's hands to escape her peril. Her muffled screams could barely be heard as she fought for every breath of air. Her head was turning slightly from side to side, but the child had a good grip and her face was still forced hard into the airbag.

In blind panic, Sarah managed to reach around to the back of her head and pull at the evil boy's fingers to try and prise them off. This added challenge seemed to please the urchin, which made him smile, showing some dirty, blackened teeth. He then plunged his fang-like teeth into Sarah's hand, and the muffled yells of his victim grew a bit louder. The demonic boy bit harder and harder and moved his head from side to side, and a loud cracking was heard as some fingers were ripped off and streams of deep red blood shot up and splashed all around the interior of the car and onto the boy's face. The stubs where the fingers once were poured with blood and horrible loose flesh hung from the gaping holes. Sarah moved her painful hand back onto the airbag, which turned the white pillow red, and the evil brat stood up outside the car, still holding the doomed woman's face deep into the airbag.

The boy chewed Sarah's severed fingers for a few seconds then spat them out onto the ground. With an evil grin he pushed her head deeper and harder into her airbag, and the near-dead woman began to shake. Her feet instinctively kicked out, smashing into the pedals, dislocating her ankles and twisting them both in a gruesome and repulsive way. The bones of her feet were sticking out through the skin, and the boy saw a last chance to inflict more pain on his prey.

He reached down and grabbed one of the protruding bones and started to twist and turn it, and with each cracking twist it made Sarah convulse and shake even more in agony. Her end was near. The boy let out an evil chuckle, and with one last thrust of her head and pulling of bone, Sarah's body became rigid. Then it relaxed and was still; she suffered no more.

Her arms flopped down by her sides and the boy released his grip. He stood up and let out a disappointed sigh, knowing his evil pleasure was over. The Entertainer then walked up and stood behind him and lovingly put his hand on his offspring's shoulder.

"Well done, my son," he said in admiration at the boy's evil work. "Well done."

The Entertainer then removed the King of Clubs playing card from the ribbon around his hat, but as before, the same card remained in the hatband. It seemed like there was an infinite number of cards at his disposal.

He placed the card on the back of Sarah's head, still embedded in the airbag, turned and walked away, followed by his loyal young servant. They walked to the bushes at the roadside and vanished into them, leaving the horrendous sight to be discovered by some unlucky person who would happen to stumble upon the gruesome scene.

RANDOMS

The next afternoon at the police station, Josh, Maggie and Steve were trying to piece together the details of the strange deaths to see what they could discover. There were pictures of the deceased pinned on a large board on the wall with bits of paper with notes on them which were all relevant to the case. A constable knocked on the door and walked in.

"Here's that info you needed, guv," he said to Steve, handing him a piece of paper.

Steve nodded as he took the paper from him and the constable left the room. He read the note and pinned it onto the board, then turned to Josh and Maggie, who were both sitting at a table.

"Well," Steve said with a sigh, "we have a firm connection to go with our King of Clubs card."

He sat down with his two friends, and an excited Maggie asked, "Well, what is it, then?"

Steve looked at Maggie, then turned to Josh and said, "It seems more of our victims used to go out with each other when they were younger."

He got up and walked back to the incident board. He read the latest note and announced to Josh and Maggie, "Louise used to go out with Tony, Alan used to date Michelle, and Sarah, our latest death, was George's girlfriend when they were teenagers. Michelle and Alan were still friends but the other four just lost contact, as you do over the years, and hadn't seen each other for over fifteen years or so. This has to mean something, but what?"

An uneasy silence filled the room as they all tried to get some inspiration from somewhere. Suddenly the silence was broken.

"Could it be jealous ex-partners?" Maggie suggested.

Steve shook his head. "No, that just doesn't sound right."

There was a short pause while they all thought for more ideas, then Josh blurted out, "I know – it could be an old friend with a grudge."

Maggie nodded, but Steve disagreed.

"Yes, but that would only work if they all had the same friend. No, it must be something else."

They sat there, defeated and devoid of ideas, when Maggie suddenly shot up out of her seat.

"Children!" she shouted.

"My God, Maggie," Josh sighed "You scared the living daylights out of me."

He sighed again as Steve replied to Maggie, "Children – what do you mean?"

Maggie went up to the board and pointed to some of the pictures. "Don't you see? A witness said he thought he saw a young boy in the seat of the roller that killed

George, but he couldn't be totally sure and Louise's husband told us he heard her groan the word 'child' just before she died."

Maggie scanned the board again. "Look here," she exclaimed, "the passer-by who found Sarah swore he saw a youth near to where her car was, but when he got to Sarah the boy had gone. There were the fresh footprints of a child in the field where Michelle was found too. It seems the potential sighting of children at the scenes is only fleeting, but why?"

She then sat back down and whispered, "I also felt the evil presence of what could have been a child in the bank just after Alan's death. This has to be it."

Steve nodded in agreement. "You could be on to something, Maggie, well done."

Josh chimed in and voiced his concern. "Yes, but where have these children come from and where did they all go?"

"Well, we can't find out too much in here," Steve stated. "Come, let's go into town and investigate further and see what else we can find out."

They all agreed and left the room to see what else they could discover.

***

Elsewhere, in an unnaturally cold and misty field a few short miles out of town, ghostly music could be heard and the sound of evil laughter and song rang out through the air. The field was full of apparitions and spirits of people long gone. Mixed in with the crowd were the Entertainer's children, and the Entertainer himself was walking through the flock.

A rock band were performing on an old wooden stage near the edge of the field, and the words *STATE OF EXIT* were written in blood above them. This was clearly the name of the band, who were belting out loud music to a lively and rowdy audience as the blood gushing from their name flowed out further and further and started to run out onto the boards of the stage.

With a closer look you could see that the four band members were all chained together and they were in a tortured, zombie-like state, but they did sound great, which is probably why the Entertainer chose them as his personal entertainment.

The drummer was banging away the beat and blood splashed up from the drum skins, soaking him and his drums in a deep red coating. The bass player kept the rhythm, but as he played the skin was being burnt off his fingers by the red-hot strings of his guitar. The lead guitarist strummed a blistering riff, but screamed in pain as the guitar lead around his throat tightened with every note he played.

The singer was also playing backing guitar and belting out the words to a song about being a zombie, dead inside, but his words were strained as his guitar was on fire and he was singing through his agony. However, the whole band seemed perfectly at home despite their pains, performing to their spectral audience and they fitted in superbly with the ghostly surroundings. Their music seemed to make the crowd even more noisy and boisterous, but the Entertainer's children were bored. They all walked up to the Entertainer and looked at him. They never said a word; they didn't have to as the Entertainer knew what they wanted.

"Ah, OK, my family," he said as he spread out his hands to them. "I sense your frustration and boredom continue."

He pointed a bony finger and added, "Go and have some extra fun."

The ghostly children all beamed and ran off in different directions, disappearing into the dusk.

The Entertainer turned to the rock band and shouted, "Play on, louder!"

This made the crowd roar and cheer, and State of Exit continued to blast out their rock music.

***

Two of the evil children, a girl and a boy, were now in another field where they saw a local farmer on his combine harvester. They smiled at each other and ran through the crops towards him.

The farmer saw them and furiously yelled at them, "Keep away, there are dangerous things here!"

But the children ran closer and closer. Suddenly the sinful girl tripped and fell into the rotating machine's blades. The farmer screamed and he saw blood and body parts fly out from the front of his harvester. An arm and a leg were thrown through the air and blood-splattered lumps of flesh were hurled all around.

"No!" he yelled as he turned off the engine and climbed down. "I told you both to keep away!"

The evil boy just stood there and watched as the farmer went to examine the blades to see what was left of the poor child. He was stunned as he saw the bloodied remains of the girl still lodged in between the blades of his machine. He couldn't mutter a word due to the horror of what he had just done. He raised his hand towards the girl's body to try to remove her, and as he touched her head the child's eyes shot wide open and gave out a cold, black stare. This made the farmer fall back in shock, and he just sat there on the ground, looking at her in disbelief.

"No, that's impossible," he uttered to himself.

He shook his head, thinking he was imagining it all, and slowly raised his gaze back up to the girl, but she was still looking straight at him. She was entwined around the sharp rotor blades of the wheel with her remaining arm and leg mangled in the wreckage. Half of the top of her head was missing and her intestines were flopping out from her stomach.

Suddenly her stare became more intense and she started to laugh at the poor farmer. It wasn't a quiet, nervous laugh but a loud, evil one, and she didn't stop. She just laughed and laughed at the farmer, oblivious to her own plight. The farmer rose to his feet in shock; he couldn't believe what he was seeing. He rubbed his eyes and looked again, but this time, the girl was gone.

Before he could say or do anything, the machine's engine started up and the large bladed wheel began to turn and spin again. He looked into the cab and saw the boy sitting in the seat.

He frantically shouted to the child, "Get down from there and turn it off!"

The boy didn't respond, and then the farmer heard a noise directly behind him. He turned around, and to his horror he saw the young girl standing there, fully intact.

The farmer opened his mouth and took in a large breath, but he didn't know it was to be his last one. The wretched girl lunged at him and pushed him backwards into the blades of the combine harvester. There seemed to be a slight pause as the doomed farmer's eyes widened with fright, but then it was all over. He was ripped to shreds on the blades and his arms and legs were flung over the field as the rest of his body was chopped into small pieces of gruesome flesh. Blood and guts rained down and his bloody, sliced-up head was tossed out and landed at the feet of the young girl, who placed a Joker playing card on the forehead as the King of Clubs card was saved exclusively for the Entertainer's revenge related deaths and not for random ones. The boy then turned off the machine and the two diabolical reprobates walked away hand in hand.

***

Not too far away in an old farmyard along the coast road was a blacksmith's Forge which was still in use, and Ashley, the blacksmith, was working away, hammering on the anvil. He was making some horseshoes, but he didn't seem happy with the one he was working on. He walked over to the grinding wheel and turned it on. He started to grind away at the horseshoe when he became aware of someone behind him. He spun around to see an ashen youth standing there dressed in rags.

The youth quickly and violently grabbed Ashley by the head and pushed his face onto the still-spinning grinder. Ashley screamed in agony as sparks flew out from the wheel and his face was ripped to shreds. There was a sickening crack as his nose broke and was bent to the side. He was just about to pass out when the youth let go and Ashley fell to the floor, clutching his hot, smouldering face. The demonic boy looked around the forge to see what else he could do to the damned blacksmith.

He saw hammers of different weights and size, sharp chisels, chains and a seven-foot-long trough full of red-hot ashes. This pleased the urchin, and he easily picked up the pained forger and threw him into the burning embers.

Ashley thrashed about in the hot ashes. He was being burnt alive; it was like being tossed into a volcano. As he fought to escape the trough, the fiery embers and ashes were tossed up into the air in a whirlpool of fire. Suddenly, the evil boy grabbed Ashley and pulled him out of the burning trough, throwing him to the ground. Ashley couldn't move as he was in too much agony. His body looked like it was covered in a fiery coat of hot sand and his blistered skin was melting off with the intense heat.

The youth then spread out Ashley's arms and legs, and with Ashley now spread-eagled on the floor, the ghastly boy got four horseshoes and, with the help of a lump hammer, pinned Ashley's arms and legs firmly to the ground. Ashley was now at the mercy of this demon child and through his pain he managed to open his eyes, but he soon wished he hadn't.

The youth was standing over him, holding the heavy anvil high above his head, and Ashley knew what was to come. He tried to wriggle free, but he was firmly pinned by the strong iron horseshoes.

With his white teeth now showing through his burnt-away lips, Ashley managed to mumble, "No", but it was to no avail.

The wicked degenerate stood directly over the prone blacksmith's head and dropped the anvil. The heavy iron block smashed and crushed Ashley's skull as if it was made of glass. Pieces of bone, sinew and brain just managed to shoot out before the anvil embedded itself firmly into the floor. A red corona could be seen on the floor around the base of the anvil containing blood, tissue and a detached eyeball; it was a horrible, gruesome death. The boy then placed a Joker card on top of the anvil and happily walked out of the shed, knowing that his work was done.

***

All of the Entertainer's children returned to the field and each of them looked happy; there was no telling what evil deeds they had just completed. The Entertainer then shouted, "The show is now over – go back home to Midway!"

State of Exit stopped playing and then got violently

pulled off the stage by a very large, muscular woman who led them away, and as they walked off they stumbled, still chained together and pained from their tortured performance. The crowd turned and walked towards what was the back of the field where they all faded out of sight, leaving the Entertainer and his clan all alone.

"Come, my children," he said lovingly to them. "We still have lots of work to do."

BOOTH

Later that same evening, Jimmy was walking down the main road of Mablethorpe. He was a bit bored, and for some reason he felt the strong urge to go into the arcade to have some fun. He looked all around the arcade and saw the usual games and slot machines. He was thinking of what to go on when his mobile went off. He took it from his pocket and read the text message; it was from his wife and she wanted to know if he had any romantic ideas for their anniversary. Jimmy phoned his wife, and smiled as she answered.

"Hello, it's me," he said. He nodded in response to what his wife was saying and then continued, "It's not until tomorrow, and yes, I do have some ideas so don't worry." Jimmy nodded again. "OK, dear, I'll see you later."

He put his phone back into his pocket and sighed. "There must be something I can do," he muttered to himself. It was obvious that he didn't really know what to get his wife for their anniversary.

He looked around the arcade and his gaze stopped

at the artist's booth. It was one of those booths that you sat in and your photo was taken, then the image was automatically drawn in the style you chose – chalk, comical, sepia etc.

Jimmy's face lit up. "That'll do – I'll get her a funny picture of me done and put it in a frame; she'll like that. She always says I look stupid."

With his mind made up, Jimmy walked up to the artist's booth and sat down on the stool. He drew the curtain for privacy and began to choose the style of picture he wanted. He put some money into the slot as the machine requested and sat there waiting for his picture to be taken.

Suddenly he felt an evil presence and had the feeling he wasn't alone, so he slowly looked down to the floor. He was shocked to see a young boy and girl sitting by his feet. They looked about eight years old and they were both very pale and grey.

"How did you get in here?" he asked the two urchins, but before they could answer, Jimmy fumed, "Go on, get out of here, you brats."

The two kids stood up and Jimmy thought they were going to leave, but he was so wrong. They suddenly and violently leapt at him, the girl squeezing his throat and the boy holding his head between his unusually strong young hands and crushing his skull. The girl then put her hand into Jimmy's mouth, ripped out his tongue, and threw it onto the floor. This was to prevent her prey from screaming.

Jimmy's eyes widened in sheer fright and blood spurted

from his mouth and ran down his shirt. His skull made a sickening cracking sound, but then the evil boy released his grip and Jimmy slumped down onto the stool as his body relaxed.

Jimmy was breathing in short, hard gasps. His expression changed from one of fright into blind terror as he saw the fingernails of both of his malicious tormentors grow to about three inches in length and become razor-sharp. His short breaths suddenly stopped as he dreaded to think about what was to happen next, but he didn't have to wait too long.

The girl plunged her cold, sharp fingers deep into Jimmy's stomach and his body became rigid once more with agony as she twisted and turned her hand deep into her victim's soft, fleshy tissue. A horrific squelching was heard as the girl pulled out her hand, and she was holding some of Jimmy's intestines and parts of his stomach in her blood-soaked palm. Her accomplice, the foul, vile boy, stood on the stool and placed his left hand on the top of Jimmy's head, and as he did so he pushed his fingernails into Jimmy's skull, piercing the very bone. With his free right hand, the brat put the nail of his index finger onto the doomed man's forehead and, with dreadful ease, like a knife through hot butter, began to move his razor talons around Jimmy's brow. The cut was deep. It was so deep it sliced the top of Jimmy's head off, and the boy took great delight in peeling the top of his skull back to reveal a soft, throbbing brain.

With one last surge of energy Jimmy tried to escape, and he kicked his legs out in front of him, which activated the photo machine and made the camera flash. However, this didn't help and the twin repulsive infants started to dig at Jimmy's brain with their sharp fingers. With each flash of the camera they scooped up pieces of brain, and blood jetted up and splashed the ceiling of the photo booth, then rained back down on them all. But this didn't stop the ghostly offspring and they just carried on tearing at Jimmy's brain and eating pieces of it. With each flash of light, blood and tissue flew; a razor-hand thrashed at more brain; more meat shoved into small, ghastly mouths; but as the deep red blood ran down their mouths and faces, Jimmy moved no more; his quivering body was already dead.

The two children then just faded away and left their pathetic victim sitting on the stool with his open head, ripped-apart brain, and intestines spilling out from his stomach which had the King of Clubs playing card sticking out from the gash. Outside, a developed photograph dropped into the tray, waiting to be discovered by some unlucky person later on that day in the arcade.

***

The two evil children then reappeared inside a house just outside Mablethorpe. The sun still shone through the window and it was a beautiful evening, but that was about to change for Lisa, whose home the evil twins were hiding in.

Lisa was sitting on her sofa reading a book called *The Elementals*, and she was laughing as it was very funny. During one of her loud fits of laughter she heard a sound coming from the kitchen. Lisa stopped laughing, put down the book and went to investigate the noise.

She walked into the kitchen and saw that the small side window was open, so without thinking she closed it. Without warning the evil boy appeared, sitting in front of her on the kitchen worktop, Lisa stared at him; then he softly whispered to her, "Hello, Mummy."

Lisa shook her head, and without even asking where he had come from replied, "I'm not your mother, and who are you?"

As she asked this question, she didn't see the devilish girl kneel down in a ball behind her. The boy then shoved Lisa backwards, making her fall over the curled-up child on the floor, smashing her head as she landed. It was the type of prank you used to play on your mates at school.

With Lisa now prone on the floor of her kitchen, the two loathsome assassins could begin their dirty work. The malevolent children each grabbed two sharp knives from a block on the kitchen side. They quickly spread the arms and legs of the still-stunned woman and plunged the knives through her hands and feet, pinning her to the floor. Helpless, Lisa screamed in pain.

She slowly regained her composure and yelled as the agony of her horizontal crucifixion started to kick in. However, her ordeal had only just started. Lisa could hear the kettle boiling, and while the two demonic brats waited, they both began to violently kick Lisa in the head and stomach.

Lisa screamed with each kick, but managed to yell, "Who are you? Why are you doing this to me?"

The kettle clicked to indicate that it had boiled, and the girl picked it up. She stood over the head of her victim and muttered, in a soft and somewhat sad voice, "Mummy."

This puzzled Lisa and made her angry. "Mummy, I'm not your mummy!" she screamed at the child.

Then the boy stood by Lisa's side and looked down at her. "No, you're not, but you should've been."

He nodded to his twin sister and she knew exactly what to do. Without any hesitation at all, the black-hearted girl slowly poured the boiling water from the kettle all over Lisa's head and face. Lisa squealed in agony as the unnaturally hot water melted away her flesh. Her skin slowly and painfully peeled away, leaving behind tender red blotches all over her scalded and blistering face. The pain was so great that when she tried to scream, no sound was forced from her mouth.

The evil boy then grabbed an electric knife from the wall and knelt down beside the helpless woman. With a sinister grin he turned on the knife and started to cut Lisa in half with the pulsating blade.

Blood spurted out from the gash and sinew was flung into the air as the blade cut away at Lisa's torso, pushed by the child from her right side further along her waistline, getting closer and closer to her belly button. The girl tipped more boiling water onto the red-raw face of her sacrifice to the Entertainer, and Lisa could only force out a pathetic yelp as her agony intensified. With her face steaming and melting with the boiling heat from the water, and her body being sliced in half, she knew that she was doomed.

She became confused, but was a bit relieved, when the boy suddenly stopped cutting her when he reached her belly button. He threw the knife across the floor and looked around the kitchen.

Lisa managed to utter, "You don't have to do this. Please get me help."

The stone-cold boy then picked up the electric whisk from its wall placing and again knelt down by Lisa's side. He turned the whisk on and shoved it into her open stomach wound, holding it deep inside as the whisk spun around, cutting and chopping into Lisa's innards.

Blood was spat out from the near-dead woman's mouth, and the evil girl just laughed as her brother moved the whisk around inside his victim.

Lisa's guts and entrails were sent spinning around the kitchen and blood splattered everywhere. Pieces of her liver smashed onto the window and slid down the glass, leaving a deep red smear as her entire contents were spread around the room. Lisa's eyes were wide open; she was dead but this didn't stop the boy as he moved the whisk inside her stomach from side to side, slicing every piece of her until she was severed completely in half.

The vicious child turned off the whisk and stood up beside his sister. The girl produced the symbolic King of Clubs playing card from her pocket and placed it on Lisa's blood-soaked chest. The two demonic twins then held hands and vanished, leaving the devastating and gruesome scene, and yet another victim of these ghastly, forgotten souls.

MIDWAY

Maggie was tossing and turning in her bed as she was having a bad dream which made the sleeping psychic sweat in her turmoil. Her illusion brought forth visions of a humble village, long forgotten with the passing of time.

She saw the name *Midway* scribbled on a jagged piece of old timber; this was obviously the name of the village. In her dream she noticed that Midway was on the coast road between Mablethorpe and Ingoldmells, as she seemed to sense that she knew exactly where she was. She then realised that she was a girl, about twelve years old and a resident of the village, which was a primitive-looking place with small, quaint houses with straw roofs and thin streams of smoke rising from crude chimneys. Ducks and chickens ran around the street and horses and carts were tied in front of their owners' homes. Maggie was an avid historian and knew it must have been about 700 AD, though the exact date was not known, and the people of Midway were all walking towards a large canvas tent at the end of the main street. It looked similar to a modern day circus big top.

Maggie seemed to be caught up in the activity and found that she was walking along with the crowd. Before she knew it she was at the entrance of the marquee. To all those who could read, the sign outside read, *Come inside and experience the fantastic shows of the Entertainer.* This must have been a very popular show as all of the people seemed excited. Maggie heard one man say to his wife, "I think I'll have a go at one of them today; I feel lucky."

His wife just smiled and they hurriedly entered the tent. Maggie followed them, and inside it was very similar to what could only be described as an olden-day circus with wooden benches all around a sawdust-covered ring in the centre.

There was a musty, wet smell in the air as Maggie sat down near to the entrance, and within minutes the place was full of people. Two assistants then closed the tent flaps and the candles all around the tent were put out leaving the place in near-darkness, but you could still see what was happening as the large candles on the tables around the ring were still lit.

Suddenly, the opening to the ring itself was ablaze with fire as a candle mysteriously shot its flame high into the air. The audience all gasped with surprise and then clapped and cheered as the form of a man stood in the light. He walked forward into the centre of the ring, raised his arms and announced, in a loud, bellowing voice, "I am Bartholomew Smith, the Entertainer!"

The crowd went wild as the Entertainer continued,

"Welcome to my show. Who will be first to earn lots of money?"

Everyone in the audience rose to their feet and held their hands high in the hope that they would be picked by this strange man, who was wearing a top hat with the King of Clubs playing card tucked into the silk band and holding a silver-topped cane. This man seemed very comfortable in his surroundings and he gave the impression that he was a lot cleverer than most and he had an air of great confidence which the audience loved.

"You all know the rules," Bartholomew exclaimed. "If you survive my challenges, then you keep the money; if you don't…" He shrugged his shoulders, to the delight of the crowd, and Maggie knew that these challenges were a life-or-death gamble. This must be the entertainment they all craved.

A large wooden cage was dragged into the centre of the ring by two burly women. Three pigs were then put into the cage and the Entertainer shouted, "Who can survive three minutes in the cage with these three hungry pigs?"

Hands were thrust up into the air again, and Bartholomew pointed to a man in the crowd. The people cheered and clapped as the man walked into the ring and faced the Entertainer. The crowd fell silent as Bartholomew Smith said to the man, "What's your name, sir?"

"I am Seth, the blacksmith's son," the nervous but happy man replied.

"Well, Seth, all you have to do is stay in the cage for three minutes to win this."

He pointed to the ring's entrance, and a very large bag, obviously full of coins, was wheeled out. The crowd cheered as the Entertainer continued, "Do you accept the challenge and the rules?"

Seth looked all around the tent at his cheering fans, and with a broad grin shouted, "Yes, I do!"

The seated flock were silent as one of the strong women opened the cage door and Seth stood before it.

The Entertainer put his hand on Seth's shoulder and said, "These swine haven't been fed for three days so they will snap and bite, but I'm sure you can cope."

Seth nodded and walked into the cage and the Entertainer himself closed the door.

As soon as the door shut, the three pigs ran towards Seth, and in a hurried panic he began to run around the cage. Every few seconds a pig would nip at Seth's legs and draw blood, but it was an acceptable discomfort and Seth even began to smile at how easy this challenge was as he carried on his running. A pig jumped a bit higher and bit him in the thigh making Seth squeal in pain, so he kicked the pig across the cage, which made the watching throng cheer in delight.

Seth then saw a way to see out the remaining minutes with ease, and he climbed up the cage bars so he was out of the jumping range of the pigs. He began to punch the air in triumph, but his arrogance was to be short-lived.

The Entertainer nodded towards the entrance and four large, hungry and ferocious wild boars were led into the ring by the two women assistants. To gasps from the crowd, Bartholomew opened the cage door and the four vicious beasts were let loose inside the cage. There was a look of dread and fear on Seth's face as the door was shut and the four raging boars looked up at him. He didn't even have time to scream as they all leapt up and began their feast.

They clamped their powerful jaws onto Seth's legs and pulled him, with great ease, down to the ground. There was a ripping of flesh and the sound of cracking bone as the boars were relentless in their onslaught. Seth's mouth was wide open, and a muffled yell was forced from his lips. A tear formed in his eye as he knew his end was near. The four wild beasts were mauling his arms, legs and torso, and the skin was being pulled and shredded away from his body and quickly eaten by the hungry brutes. Sharp fangs bit down hard into Seth's leg, spurting thin trails of his blood into the air as it was ripped completely away from his waist, and as Seth lay dying, his dismembered limb was the focus of a tug of war between two of the boars.

Deep red blood was being splashed all over the shocked audience by the two wild pigs tugging at the severed leg. One woman stood up and stumbled into the ring. She fainted and fell close to the cage. A boar saw this and lunged at her. He pushed his powerful dripping snout through the bars of the cage and bit hard into the woman's skull making her head cave in with a sickening crunch. Her eyes shot out and even more blood covered the audience. One boar won the tug of war and was eating the detached leg, while the boar with the woman pulled her closer to the cage and began to chew away at her stomach. The animal bit a large gash in the woman's torso and started to eat her intestines, and as he did so, he shook his head from side to side, making her guts and liver fly out and land with a splat on the reddened sawdust floor.

The two beasts gnawing at Seth were even more vicious with their prey, and they ripped off both of his arms and flung them out over the top of the cage and into the crowd, who were morbidly cheering this carnage. Seth was long dead by now, and with razor teeth the boars devoured every part of his innards they could feast on. Blood, guts, and body parts were all strewn across the ring and tossed into the crowd, and with one last strong tug, the beasts tore Seth completely in half. The crowd screamed in horror at this bloody and violent scene, and then the Entertainer spoke.

"Enough, my pets!" he shouted, and the well-trained boars all stopped their attack and walked out of the ring, each with a body part to finish devouring outside. The two women assistants quickly brushed down the ring and all was now set for the next life-or-death challenge. Bartholomew smiled.

"Who's next for the chance of winning the money?"

Still cheering but a little less enthusiastically due to the horror they had just experienced, some members of the crowd again raised their hands, but there were a lot fewer of them than before.

"Who can skip?" Bartholomew asked, and then instantly pointed to a young girl. "Can you?"

The girl jumped eagerly into the arena as the skipping challenge was set up in the centre of the ring. There were two wooden poles about three feet high which had a skipping rope attached to them. With the pulling of a nearby wooden lever which went into the ground, the skipping rope somehow began to turn automatically.

"So you can skip, then?" he asked the girl.

She nodded, but as she didn't say anything, Bartholomew continued, "You know the rules; if you survive the skipping test you win the money on the table. Do you accept the challenge?"

The girl saw the rope turning slowly and smiled at the thought of how easy it seemed. She thought that even if the rope spun faster, she would still cope. She looked around at the cheering crowd, turned to the Entertainer and said, "Yes, I accept."

To a clapping audience, Bartholomew Smith hollered, "Let the challenge begin."

He looked at the girl and explained the conditions of the test. "All you have to do is to skip for three minutes to win; it's that easy."

The girl nodded and walked up to the turning rope. She jumped in and started to skip. She found it easy and after about one minute the crowd were getting a little bored as nothing was happening, but then things started to change.

The Entertainer announced, "My people, I forgot to tell you that it isn't actually a skipping rope; it is a skipping wire."

The crowd gasped and wondered what was planned for this young victim.

"Now, now," the Entertainer said in a confident

manner, "The rules are still the same; all she has to do is to skip."

The watching mob then noticed that the two wooden poles to which the wire was fixed had begun to rise. There must have been an underground mechanism causing this to happen but no one seemed to question this advanced machinery. The poles rose higher and higher up out of the ground, which made the wire a lot higher as well. This made skipping more difficult, and the young girl began to struggle to keep her rhythm as she had to jump higher and higher to avoid the razor-sharp wire. The wire then started to turn faster and faster, and the girl was trapped. With the wire rising higher and the rope spinning faster, she began to tire and could not continue.

The wire began to swoop and arc at a greater speed than before and with a last show of energy, the girl leapt as high as she could, but it wasn't high enough. As she jumped up, the sharp wire turned again and sliced through her legs at the knees. The bottom halves of her legs were flung out across the ring, leaving strings of thin, bloody sinew in their path.

The poor child landed upright and was balancing on the stumps where her knees once were, but before she had the chance to scream out in pain, the wire swooped around again. This time it sliced straight through her neck, beheading the unlucky volunteer. Her decapitated head spun through the air, shooting out blood all over the crowd, and landed on the table where the bag of money sat. There were screams of terror from the onlookers as they couldn't believe what they had just witnessed.

The Entertainer became a bit confused as he sensed the disapproval of the audience. They had seen his acts before so he wondered why the crowd were more rowdy than usual. The Entertainer then shouted, "They all knew the rules and accepted the challenges." To loud boos, he added, "This show is now over – see you all next time!"

Despite this slight unrest from the crowd he sensed that they would be back; if not in this village, then in other ones, as people always wanted to win money.

The two burly women walked out into the ring, each holding two of the wild boars on strong leather straps, and the Entertainer left the ring as the crowd vacated the tent.

Suddenly Maggie found herself witnessing the forming of a lynch mob in what was the main street of Midway. There were about twenty or more in the rabble, and some of them held lit torches while the others had pitchforks, shovels, or any other weapon they could get. The village's elder, Mr Cedric Hannah, whose daughter had just been killed by the skipping device, was crying as he led the mob up to a house at the end of the street. The crowd faced the house and the elder shouted, "No mercy – burn the demons!"

The mob all yelled out and threw their lit torches onto the roof of the house. The straw quickly caught fire. A man then said "Mr Hannah, shall we burn the inside as well?"

Cedric nodded, and the door was broken down by the mob and more torches were thrown inside the house. A woman's screams were heard from inside – "No, my children!" but the lynch mob didn't care as they watched the house burn and listened to the people inside perish to tragic screams and wails.

From a short distance away, a shout was heard; it was the Entertainer himself, and he yelled from a type of crow's nest at the top of his marquee, "No, what have you done to my family!"

A voice rang out from the crowd "Look he's there!" as fingers were pointed up to the Entertainer high above his tent.

The mob all turned and ran towards the circus tent as it was clear from their shouts that they had just torched the Entertainer's home thinking he was inside it.

They reached the marquee and Bartholomew Smith was still at the top of the tent. He had seen the smoke and flames and had climbed up to see what was happening, but he didn't expect to see his own house ablaze.

The mob set fire to the tent and the animals and assistants all ran out and sprinted off into the distance. The tent burned quickly and Bartholomew had nowhere to go; he was trapped up the main pole, high up in the air.

Knowing he was doomed, he shouted down to his murderers, "Mark my words: I curse you all and your families, and I will have my revenge. I will be back; one day I will be back!"

Then, without any hesitation at all, he just let go of the pole and fell to his death in the inferno below.

Maggie seemed to recognise some of the lynch mob, but she knew that she couldn't know them as this village existed hundreds of years ago. Then she heard the Entertainer scream out from the flames, and she woke up.

Maggie composed herself and muttered, "My God."

She took a notepad from the drawer of her bedside table and wrote down what she could remember about her vision, and as she did, she had a look of dread and foreboding on her face. Maggie knew that she had discovered something of great importance about the strange deaths.

GRIMES

Early the next morning, Maggie went to Josh's house. She knocked on the door and Rosie answered. This surprised Maggie, and she said "Oh, I'm sorry it's a bit early but I really need to speak to Josh."

Rosie didn't know who this strange necklace-covered woman was, so she called Josh to the door. He was surprised to see Maggie so early.

"Maggie!" He beamed. "Please come in."

Maggie went inside, and Josh closed the front door and introduced his guest to his wife. "Rosie, this is Maggie; I have mentioned her to you before."

The two women shook hands.

"I've heard a lot about you," admitted Rosie. "You've helped my husband quite a lot lately."

Maggie replied, with a smile, "Well, I do try to do my bit."

Rosie sensed that Josh and Maggie needed to talk about work, so she kissed Josh on the cheek and whispered into his ear, "I'll leave you two to it." She then went upstairs, and Josh led Maggie into the kitchen.

"Coffee, Maggie?"

"Yes please, I think I need one."

Josh boiled the kettle and made the drinks. They sat at the table for a while then Josh broke the silence.

"Go on then, what have you got for me?"

Maggie looked directly into Josh's eyes and said, with a slight tremble in her voice, "I had a vision last night. It was about a village called Midway and a man who called himself the Entertainer. This all happened hundreds of years ago and he had a sort of circus show where people accepted his challenges for money, but I never saw anyone actually survive the tests to collect their reward. After a young girl was killed, a lynch mob burnt his house and his circus tent to the ground and killed the Entertainer and his family."

She paused and took a sip of coffee. Josh saw his chance to speak.

"So, what does this all mean?" he asked the still-shaken psychic. "Who is the Entertainer?"

Maggie put down her cup and continued her story. "I think that the Entertainer has come back to get his revenge for the murder of his family, and is responsible for all of the strange deaths."

This stunned Josh, as he found the story unlikely. "Why do you think that?" he questioned Maggie. "How can a man long dead be alive today?"

As Josh drank his coffee, Maggie dropped her bombshell.

"The Entertainer kept a King of Clubs card in his hatband, and he cursed the lynch mob and swore he'd have his revenge. Some of the mob looked a little familiar and could be related to the victims. The man is sadistic and evil and I really do have the feeling that the Entertainer has returned."

Josh realised that his friend was deadly serious, and trusted her instincts. "OK, Maggie, if you're right then what do we do?"

Maggie was thankful that he believed her, and stood up. "We go and see old Mr Grimes the hermit; he knows about the area's history and other strange stuff."

Josh agreed and shouted up to Rosie, "I'm going out, luv; see you later!"

Rosie shouted back down and said that she'd see him when he got back, and Josh and Maggie left the house and drove to see Mr Grimes.

***

They drove up a dirt track which led to an old house that overlooked the sea. It was a spooky, untidy-looking house, a bit like the ones you can see in any horror movie. They pulled up outside and walked up an overgrown path to the front door.

"Now be aware that he doesn't like people much," Maggie warned Josh. "He likes to be left alone unless you talk about something of real interest to him."

"Well, let's hope this interests him then," a curious Josh chuckled.

Maggie was just about to knock on the door when it flew open and there stood Mr Grimes. He was an elderly man with white hair and a short beard. He was a bit scruffy-looking, and scary with it. He had an angry look on his face, and hollered at his intruders, "Get off my property – go away!"

He raised his hand in a threatening manner, which made Josh and Maggie step back.

"Wait!" Maggie shrieked. "It's me, Bill, Maggie!"

Bill Grimes blinked and took a hard look at her. "My God, Maggie, it is you."

Calm fell on the three, and as Bill ushered Maggie and Josh inside he said, "Come in, come in", and the door creaked shut behind them. He showed them into his living room and they all sat down, Maggie and Bill on the sofa and Josh in an armchair that was full of holes and needed reupholstering.

"Bill, this is Josh," Maggie said with a smile as she introduced the two men. "We've got some things to ask you."

Bill Grimes shuffled in his seat. "OK, ask away."

Maggie began the questions. "What can you tell us about an old village called Midway and a man called the Entertainer?"

Bill got up and walked over to a dusty old bookcase. He scanned his books for a few seconds and then picked one out and sat back down.

"I think what you need is in here," he mumbled as he patted his book tenderly. "There have been quite a lot of evil and malicious characters throughout the history of this area, and if I remember correctly, the Entertainer was the darkest of the lot."

He opened the book, which was full of notes, diagrams and scraps of paper. It wasn't a proper book as such; it was one that Bill had put together himself with facts and details he found interesting about history and evil in general.

He turned the pages. "Ah, here we are," he said with a lot of interest in his voice, "I knew I was right. Midway was on the coast road and existed about 700 years ago, give or take a century or two although nobody knows exactly when it was." He continued to read. "Small town... humble dwellings – ah, what's this?"

Josh and Maggie suddenly became more interested as Bill carried on reading.

"I knew it – the Entertainer, real name Bartholomew Smith."

"That's it!" shouted an excited Maggie. "Bartholomew Smith, that's who I saw in my dream"

Bill Grimes quickly raised his head and looked straight at Maggie. "Dream – what dream?"

Maggie's eyes flicked to Josh and then back to Bill. "I had a sort of vision last night. I was in Midway and I saw the Entertainer's freakish shows and the lynch mob that murdered him and his family. I heard him curse the mob and swear his revenge on all of them. He swore to return one day, and I think he's back."

Bill looked at Maggie and confessed, "I think you might be right."

"What!" Josh butted in. "How can that be?"

Bill continued with his tale. "The Entertainer was a devil worshipper and into black magic and the supernatural. No one knew who he really was or where he came from, he's a bit of a historical mystery. The lynch mob tied his charred body to horses and dragged it through the streets and out of Midway. It's said that you could hear the screams of the dead themselves as his body was battered and pulled along the roads. It's rumoured that the mob buried him close to the beach, under where the funfair now is.

"Bartholomew Smith's wife was pregnant when she was killed by the lynch mob, so he swore revenge on their families and cursed any future unborn children that the mob or their relatives may have had due to the horrific killing of his family."

Maggie and Josh were both stunned at this revelation, but things now started to fit into place.

Maggie chimed in, "Children – there were always children seen or thought to have been seen at some of the strange deaths. I'm not too sure but I thought that I caught a fleeting glimpse of a child in the bank when Alan was killed. I've also got a strong feeling that these children actually knew their victims" The frightened look on Maggie's face said it all as she looked at Josh.

"Let me get this right," a puzzled Josh remarked. "Are you thinking that these killer children are the ghostly offspring that the victims would have had if they had stayed in a relationship, but they weren't actually conceived because the couple broke up beforehand?"

The colour drained from Maggie's face. "That's exactly what I'm thinking and that's also the reason the victims used to be lovers"

There was an eerie silence as the size of the problem became clear.

Bill then made a suggestion to Josh: "You need to find exactly where Midway used to be as I think you'll uncover a few clues there. I visited the field where the village once stood about forty years ago, but I won't be able to find it again now as I didn't write down the location as I didn't think it would be that important. All I can remember is that it was near Trusthorpe, and there was a strange circle of semi-buried stones in the corner."

Josh stood up. "You stay here," he ordered Maggie. "I'll go and find the field and see what's there."

Maggie nodded, and Josh left to go on his journey of discovery, but what exactly would he find?

THE CIRCLE

Josh was driving along the coast road between Mablethorpe and Ingoldmells, trying to find the field where Midway once stood. It was a nice summer's day and he had the window down to get some breeze. He pulled up alongside a field and got out of the car.

After looking around the area for a moment, he decided to walk across the field to see if he could find the stone circle or any other clues. It wasn't a large field, and as soon as he got about halfway across he could see that there weren't any stones there or anything else at all, so he returned to his car and drove a little further down the road to the next field.

He parked next to a larger field which went back a lot further than the others along the road. He got out of the car and took a few steps onto the lush, green grass, and immediately felt uneasy. He took out a King of Clubs playing card from his pocket which he had took from a pack of cards earlier hopefully for some kind of inspiration and walked towards what he assumed was the rear of the field as it was the furthest edge away from the road. He scanned the edge of the field and his gaze was drawn to the back left corner where the grass didn't look quite as green as the rest, so he walked over to investigate. Straight away he could see why the grass was duller: it was growing over a cluster of different-sized, semi-buried stones, but they all looked similar and it was obvious that they had belonged to the same ancient building that once stood there. But what could it have been?

Josh knew that this must be the very field where Midway used to be, and to get some kind of inspiration he looked hard at the card in his hand.

Then suddenly the sun crept behind what must have been the only cloud in the sky, which made Josh become as cold as ice. Then, without any warning at all, the Entertainer appeared behind Josh and grabbed him by the shoulders, which made Josh feel faint and dizzy. As the Entertainer gave an evil smile, Josh fell, unconscious, to the ground.

***

When his eyes flickered open and he regained his composure, he sat up to see where he was. He was shocked to see that he was locked in a wooden cage, and there were people dressed in rags and olden-day clothes staring at him. He could hear what could only be described as loud crowd activity coming from behind a closed curtain. Looking around at the people outside, he thought he had to say something if he was to get out of his primitive prison.

"Where am I?" he said in a slightly raised voice. "Let me out of here!"

One of the men outside the cage was holding a pointed stick, and he thrust it through the wooden bars and stabbed Josh in his arm. It didn't penetrate too deeply, but it drew blood and made Josh reel back in pain.

He knew then that he was in danger. He looked all around to assess what was going on, but he didn't like what he saw. He knew that the old-fashioned surroundings were just too good to be replicas, and that he had somehow gone back in time. Was he dreaming or was he really there? The cut on his arm seemed real enough, and so did the intimidating atmosphere.

"Ah, you're awake at last." An evil voice pierced the air. "I'm so glad you're here."

Josh turned towards the closed curtain that masked the circus activities, and his eyes widened with fear as he saw the Entertainer standing there, as bold as brass, leaning on his cane.

An apprehensive Josh muttered, "You – what do you want with me?"

Bartholomew Smith slowly walked up to the cage and glared at his helpless prisoner. "What do I want? I want you to suffer, and to leave me and my children alone to wreak our revenge on those who did us wrong. That's what I want."

Josh saw the chance to get some information and details, so he bravely asked, "Children, revenge – what do you mean?"

The Entertainer never missed a chance to hear his own

voice, so he replied, "My children were denied the chance of life by their selfish would have been parents, so I granted them life. My family and I were murdered at the hands of their ancestors, and now I am getting the revenge that I promised would be mine, and trust me, revenge really is sweet. My mark, the King of Clubs, is the thirteenth club card, so I will have thirteen deaths as payment, apart from one or two that came from boredom."

He then tapped the bars of the cage with his silver-topped cane and continued, "You, however, have got in the way, but fear not – I may still need you. Come, come and see your task."

What he had just heard confirmed what Maggie had suspected but before Josh could say anything else, the cage was opened and he was dragged out by the two burly women, with the crowd all cheering as he was led out through the curtain and into the main circus ring.

In the centre of the ring was a large, circular cage that was raised up about a foot from the ground. High above the cage and hanging from the ceiling, Josh saw a network of razor-sharp spikes, all eagerly waiting to come crashing down and impale whoever was unlucky enough to be inside the cage. Josh knew that he would be that person; however, he noticed that some of the spaces between the bars were wider and big enough to run out through.

He was then bundled into the cage and the door was slammed shut behind him, trapping him in one of the Entertainer's evil contraptions. Josh got to his feet, but was unsteady as the whole cage wobbled and slowly turned. He then realised why the cage was a foot off the ground: it spun round on a central pivot underneath the floor like a large child's spinning top toy. He stumbled to the edge and held on to the bars to become steady. Through the bars of the cage Josh saw the cheering crowd, all keen to see what was going to happen next; men, women and children all eagerly waiting to witness his demise.

He saw one child with a yellow flower in her hair she must have only been about four years old and he couldn't believe that her parents were letting her witness this event, but this was the entertainment of the day.

The Entertainer walked into the ring, and as he spoke, the two women started to slowly turn the cage.

"Now, my people, the next test begins!" he announced as the crowd went wild. "Can this man survive the cell of doom?"

There were shouts of "No!" and "Just kill him now!" from the horrid audience as the cage was spun around.

The Entertainer walked up to the cage and spoke to Josh. "All you have to do is run out of the cage when it stops spinning before the spikes come down on you. Easy, isn't it?"

Josh didn't speak; he knew there would be a catch or a trick somewhere.

The Entertainer then raised his arms high and shouted "Let the test begin!"

The crowd shouted louder as the two women spun the cage a bit quicker. Josh closed his eyes, but he was still getting dizzy and knew he'd have to keep his wits about him to survive this and also that there would be a trick involved. While the cage was spinning and Josh was getting dizzier, some other aides wheeled out some spikes which were attached to boards, and placed them outside the cage behind where some of the larger gaps on the edge of the cage would stop, so if Josh ran out of the wrong exit, he would be impaled. Special mirrors slid out from between the bars and covered the spaces in between them so Josh couldn't see out; he could only see what the mirrors reflected.

These strange mirrors somehow reflected images of the crowd behind them who were outside the cage and Josh had to try to find the only safe way out, Josh knew that he would be confused by the false reflections of the crowd and that he had got to work out the real exit. The cage turned faster and faster and the crowd clapped as the spikes started their descent from the ceiling. When they had reached the top of the cage, the Entertainer gave the signal for the cage to stop spinning. One of the women pressed a pedal in the floor and the cage came to an abrupt and violent halt.

Josh was thrown from the relative safety of the bars and was sent flying into the centre of the cage. He stood up, and through the bars of the larger gaps he saw what he thought was the crowd, but it was really the reflection on the mirrors coming from the false exits. He looked up and saw that the spikes were about a foot above his head, and he knew that he only had seconds to run out of the cage however he was confused, which reflections were false and which was the real exit?

The crowd all clapped and cheered, and the Entertainer shouted, "Come on, run out – you've not a lot of time, my friend!"

Josh was dizzy and didn't really know which exit to choose, and the watching crowd wanted to see him run out of a wrong exit and be killed by the waiting spikes.

The noise was deafening and confusing, and the crowd were shouting and stamping their feet as the Entertainer bellowed, "Choose quick, run out!"

The spikes were about to scrape the top of Josh's head. He started to run at one of the exits, but it was the wrong one. However, just before he ran out to be killed by the razor-sharp spikes, he suddenly stopped. He looked around, and as he became less disorientated he realised that the crowd he could see through the bars all looked identical. He then realised that they were in fact reflections in a mirror, but he still had to find the correct exit, and fast!

The deadly spikes were now so low that Josh had to stoop a little; he knew he had to make a choice. He looked around the circumference of the cage and his gaze stopped at the little girl he saw earlier who had the yellow flower in her hair. He remembered that she wore the flower on the left side of her head.

Josh quickly spun his head all around the edge of the cage, and in every image the girl had the flower on the right side of her head, so he knew that these were all reflections. The spikes were getting lower and lower and Josh was almost on his hands and knees when he finally saw the girl and the yellow flower on the left side. Now he knew that he must be looking at the real girl through the real exit.

Without any further hesitation, he ran as fast as he could and dived out of the exit to safety as the spikes came slamming down into the ground. He looked up at the girl with the flower in her hair and gave her a big smile. What he didn't see was the Entertainer standing behind him.

The Entertainer hit Josh over the head with his cane, and when Josh regained consciousness, he was back in the field where Midway once stood, and back in his own time, but he now knew a lot more of the Entertainer and his evil plans.

DUST TO DUST

The next morning Dawn was at home doing the housework. She was dusting the various ornaments that stood on small tables and sideboards in her large old manor house. There was a grand staircase in the centre of the hallway with a very large and impressive crystal chandelier hanging from the ceiling. Dawn looked up at it.

"Damn it, I hate cleaning you," she said to herself while looking at the mass of expensive glass hanging high above her.

She picked up a long handle and attached the duster to the end. Letting out a long, hard sigh, Dawn climbed up the stairs and walked along the landing. She peered over the banister at the staircase below; it seemed even higher to her from where she stood and she never did like that particular spot, but it was the best place to stand in order to actually reach the chandelier.

Dawn stood as close to the banister as she could and leant over the staircase, stretching out the duster to clean the light fitting. The duster, although extended by the long pole and Dawn's outstretched arm, only just reached the crystal, and it was softly tickling the sparkling glass. Dawn hated this task, but it had to be done.

As the crystal turned slightly, the sun reflected off it and shone directly into Dawn's eyes. Dawn stepped back and shook her head. She didn't see the shape of a young girl, about eleven years of age, forming at the bottom of the stairs, starting out very faint but quickly becoming more solid.

The girl was a deathly shade of grey and dressed in old clothing which had seen better days. She had long dark hair which looked like it hadn't been brushed for a month, and ripped canvas like shoes on her cold, thin feet. The mischievous child also had a piece of thick cord wrapped a few times around her slim waist for a belt. The girl slowly began to climb up the stairs with her thin hand softly dragging along the handrail behind her.

Dawn composed herself, and once again she stretched out over the long drop above the stairs to clean the chandelier, but then she saw the ghostly figure of the girl climbing up. Dawn screamed and stepped backwards onto the landing. She started to tremble and was scared stiff at what she had just seen. She put both of her hands over her open mouth and breathed deeply. Calming herself, she muttered, "No – it must have been a trick of the light."

Getting her nerve back, Dawn walked back to the railing and slowly looked down the stairs. There was no sign of the ghostly child, just the glint of sunlight shining off the overhanging chandelier. Dawn sighed once again.

"I really hate these damn stairs," she whispered to herself.

She picked up the long duster, but this time she didn't just lean over the banister; she actually climbed over it to be able to reach out further to access a few more of the crystals. It was a dangerous position to be in, but she had done it many times before.

"Let's get this over with," she said with a shake of her head.

Dawn held on to the banister with her left hand while stretching out as far as she could with the duster in her right hand. She was smiling as she cleaned, probably thinking about the ghost she didn't really see, but as we all know, the child was really there and she did see her. The girl was in fact now standing on the landing, watching her victim leaning out over the dangerous drop. With an evil grin, the girl slowly walked towards Dawn, who was now singing, oblivious to her imminent demise. Dawn leant out as far as she could and the duster was making the crystals clatter softly against each other, giving out a sound like that of a wind chime swinging in the breeze.

It was then that Dawn's singing stopped and she became aware of someone watching her. Turning her head, she saw the ghost child she had seen earlier, which made her let out a sharp yelp of surprise. Realising her precarious position, Dawn knew she had to do something and although she was terrified, she had to give the impression that she was in control.

"Who are you?" the scared woman asked the urchin. "What are you doing here?"

The young girl then walked over and stood opposite Dawn, on the other side of the banister. She looked directly into Dawn's face and opened her mouth unnaturally wide. Her long, unkempt hair started to writhe about in the air, and then the child gave an ear-piercing shrill which made Dawn stumble in fright, but she managed to grip the banister to prevent a fatal fall onto the stairs below.

Dawn was still holding the long-handled duster, and she plucked up some courage and raised it above her head. She screamed at the spiteful degenerate, "Get away! Get out of my house!" But this only pleased the sinister offspring more as she saw Dawn's fright.

The child suddenly lunged forward and pushed Dawn away from the banister, but Dawn was lucky. She didn't fall to a crashing death on the stairs because as she was pushed back, her arms swung in the air and the long duster got caught up in the chandelier.

Dawn was hanging in mid-air high above the drop down onto the staircase by the duster lodged in the crystals. She screamed as her hands slipped down the handle as she knew she wouldn't survive the drop if she let go. She gripped the handle as tight as she could and her knuckles turned white. Dawn knew that her only chance of survival was the strange, pale young girl.

"I don't know who you are but please help me."

The child then removed the cord from around her waist and tied a loop at the end. She tossed it towards Dawn to try to pull her in, but she failed.

"Try again," a more hopeful Dawn said. "This time I'll try to grab it."

The girl was ready to try again, and Dawn carefully took one hand away from the duster handle. Her grip was failing and she slipped down to the very end of the handle.

"Quick, hurry!" the frightened woman yelled. "I can't hold on much longer."

The youngster then spun the cord around her head like a cowgirl with a lasso, and with an evil smile she again tossed it towards Dawn. But she wasn't throwing it at Dawn's outstretched hand; she was aiming for her head. The cord flew through the air and went over Dawn's head, landing around her neck. The wicked brat pulled it tight around and then tied her end to the railings, stood back and waited. You could see the warped nestling longing for her victim's grip to fail, and she didn't have to wait for too long.

Dawn was gasping for air as the cord slowly drained her breath, and panic set in. She grabbed at the bond around her throat and tried to loosen it while still holding on to the duster with her other hand. She had started to swing and sway in the air, but her grip remained. Dawn was actually freeing herself from the cord and her other hand tightened even more around the end of the handle, but the evil child still looked on with stone-cold eyes, knowing the end was near.

The duster suddenly slipped from the chandelier, sealing Dawn's fate. She swung down through the air, but she didn't fall onto the stairs below as the cord remained tied to the railings above and also to her neck.

Dawn's eyes widened with fear as she swooped through the air waiting for the sickening jerk of the cord.

There was a horrible crack as the cord became taut and her slender neck was snapped. Dawn was hanging from the banister and her lifeless hands slowly slipped away from the cord around her throat, leaving the hangman's scene to be discovered by the next unfortunate person to enter the manor house.

The beaming child expertly spun a King of Clubs playing card towards Dawn's suspended corpse and it landed perfectly on her angled head, yet another victim of the Entertainer's demonic family.

BLIND

Eddie and his wife Jane had finished doing their weekly shopping and had just dumped six heaving carrier bags full of groceries onto the hallway floor.

"You go and run your bath; I'll put this lot away," Eddie said to Jane, kissing her on the cheek.

She smiled and teased, "Why, what are you after, then?"

With a broad grin on his face, Eddie quipped, "There's football on tonight, so you've got the TV in the bedroom."

"Ah, that's it," Jane chuckled. "I knew there was something."

She ran up the stairs for her bath and Eddie looked at the carrier bags.

"No problem; I'll do it in one," he whispered to himself. He then grabbed three bags in each hand and took them into the kitchen, putting them on the side.

He glanced out of the kitchen window, which overlooked an impressive garden. There was a nice wooden shed at the bottom and a long stone path running down the centre. Well-kept lawns lay on either side of the path and colourful flowers had been planted carefully all around the edge of the garden. Eddie sighed and smiled. It was a warm evening and the sun still shone, bringing out the rainbow of colours all over the garden.

Then he heard a rustle coming from outside, so he put his face nearer to the glass and peered out into the garden. But he couldn't see anything amiss.

"I knew I heard something," he muttered, so he went into the dining room where the window was larger to get a better look outside. Eddie pulled up the Venetian blind and saw a young girl in the garden. Unknown to him it was the same young girl that had killed Dawn earlier that day. Not realising that the child was pale and in rags, he banged on the window.

"Go on, get out!" he yelled, but the girl just stood there staring at him with a sad look on her face.

Eddie glanced away to get the back-door key, and as he looked back up, the girl had vanished. This puzzled him as he could see the entire garden but there was no sign of the young intruder. He laughed and shouted up to Jane, "Hey, luv, I think I've just seen a ghost!" But Jane didn't reply; she couldn't hear him due to the running bathwater.

Still smiling and a little relieved, Eddie went closer to the window and looked around the garden, where all was as it should be. He shook his head and was just about to turn away when the young girl suddenly shot up, inches away from Eddie's face on the other side of the glass. She must have been crouching down below the window, but Eddie was sure that if she had been there he would've still seen her which puzzled him. This time he did realise that the malevolent kid was deathly pale and scruffy-looking. Eddie still wasn't sure if she was a ghost or not, so he again shouted, "Get out, go on!"

The unpleasant child then took a few steps backwards down the garden path. Her gaze still firmly fixed on Eddie she raised both of her arms above her head.

Suddenly, Eddie became frightened as the atmosphere became freezing cold and had an eerie feeling all around it. He didn't speak or shout at the girl; he couldn't open his mouth or make a sound due to the immense feeling of fear and dread. The hateful young girl then stretched out her arms either side of her sickly thin body, which made an unholy wind start up that blew all of the flower heads off and scattered them over the lawn. The wind blew through the girl's untidy hair, giving the image of an evil Medusa with writhing snakes squirming from her head. Eddie was petrified, but he found the nerve to slowly walk backwards into the centre of the room where he stood still, peering out of the window.

Although he was standing in the middle of the dining room, he could still see the ghastly child in his garden and the wind was getting stronger. Eddie summoned up all of his strength, paced over to the window and quickly dropped the Venetian blind. He retraced his backwards steps into the centre of the room and stood staring at the lowered blind. He did feel a bit safer. He could still see the child through the open slats, but at least he was inside and this strange, ghostly mite was still outside.

Then Eddie jumped as the Venetian blind started to

rattle and shake. It began to ripple in the unnatural breeze from outside that had somehow found its way into the dining room, but the breeze was silent and localised around the blind.

Eddie started to breathe a little faster, and the Venetian blind began to shake and flap more violently than before. It was flying about and banging on the window frame and the wind was more intense, but then it came to an abrupt stop and all was silent. Eddie sighed – was his ordeal now at an end?

He took a step towards the window, but then the violent wind suddenly started up again. Before Eddie could take another step, the Venetian blind came flying off the wall and shot straight towards him. The blind hurtled at the rigid man and sliced through him from the knees upwards. Some fingers dropped to the ground and his right hand fell onto the wooden floor of the dining room. Still he stood there as if nothing had happened. He was obviously dead, all of his organs now sliced into inch-thick pieces, but his sticky body fluids must have kept him upright.

Jane then walked in and saw her husband just standing there in the centre of the room.

"What are you doing there?" the unsuspecting woman asked, but Eddie didn't reply.

Before Jane could say or do anything else, the strain on Eddie's body became too much and his sliced-up corpse started to spread and collapse to the floor. Each slice of his body slid either to the left or to the right, like a sliced banana or slices of ham being cut by a butcher, making a disgusting squelching sound as they slid apart. Jane screamed as her husband collapsed into a mound of inch-thin parts and his scarlet blood ran all over the floor, forming a massive puddle. She fainted, but just before she lost consciousness she thought she caught a glimpse of an evil child, now standing in the room. Eddie's body settled, stacked on the floor, looking like a giant pack of bloodied playing cards.

With an evil grin all over her face, the ghastly urchin walked over to the blood-soaked mound that was once Eddie and placed the King of Clubs card on top of her sliced-up victim.

Bartholomew Smith, the Entertainer, then appeared behind his demonic offspring, patted her on the shoulder and spoke.

"Nice job, well done."

They then faded away, leaving the carnage behind.

NIGHT SHIFT

The next day, Josh, Maggie and Steve were in the incident room of the police station. Josh had told Steve and Maggie about his adventure back in time to Midway, and Maggie told Steve about her vision. Steve told them both about Dawn's death and his early-morning visit to Eddie's house and the carnage left behind, and things were slowly beginning to fit into place and make more sense. Steve stood up and walked over to the incident board, which had more photos and details pinned to it than before.

"OK, let me get this right," a shocked Steve began. "We have the ghost of a man called Bartholomew Smith, known as the Entertainer, who has evil children killing who would have been their parents."

Josh and Maggie looked at each other as they realised just how stupid it all sounded.

"I know," a bewildered Josh sighed, "It does sound like something from a horror story, but it all seems to fit."

Maggie jumped to her feet and banged on the table. "I know it's true!" she shouted, fearing Steve was having doubts. "Please believe us; I have had dreams and visions and Josh has actually been in Midway."

She sat back down and Steve joined them at the table. He fumbled with some papers and announced what he thought.

"OK, don't worry." Steve shook his head. "Strange as it may seem, I do believe we've got some supernatural events happening here, and now we've got to deal with them. The connections are too great to ignore – the King of Clubs, the ex-boyfriends and girlfriends, the ghostly children, Midway and the Entertainer – but what to do?"

The three were all sitting and thinking about what their next course of action could be.

"We've got to get a step in front of the Entertainer, but how?" Maggie mused. "How do we know where he's going to strike next?"

Josh stood up, walked over to the window and looked out. He didn't turn around when he spoke. "We've got to wait for the next death."

A puzzled Maggie replied, "What do you mean?"

Steve fidgeted in his seat, waiting for Josh's answer as he himself wasn't sure how this was going to pan out.

Josh turned and faced them. "It's obvious," he continued. "After the next death, we have to find the victim's past lovers and protect them from the Entertainer's children. That's how we get a step in front."

Steve nodded. "It's a big ask, but I've got some good men on the case and we'll do our best."

Josh sat back down and voiced more concern. "Bartholomew Smith said there would be thirteen deaths in revenge for him and his family, but that's an odd number. Surely if these devil children are killing whoever would have been their parents, there should be an even number of deaths: one for each mother and father. Anyway, we've had ten deaths so far, so if the worst comes to the worst there are only three more and then it should be over."

"You're right," Steve butted in, "but we've still got to try to prevent the last killings. OK, we can't do much now so we've no choice but to wait for the next death."

They all sat there with a look of impending defeat on their faces as they knew there wasn't much they could do and it was building up to a gruesome ending. Little did they know that they didn't have to wait much longer for the next gruesome death as the Entertainer had already set his sights on the next poor victim of his plan.

***

Later on that same night in a superstore, Paul was doing a night shift. He was arranging various boxes in the racking of the warehouse and the noise of the forklift trucks could be heard coming from the yard outside. The air was pierced by the beeping of a reversing lorry getting ready to be unloaded, and Paul sighed as he knew it meant even more racking away for him.

The warehouse was a bit dusty and had the usual type of racking in it. There were pallets on the floor under the shelving and in between the bars of the racks.

A child's giggle was heard, which made Paul quickly stand up, and as he had been bent over placing a box on a pallet under the racking, he banged his head on the shelf above.

"Damn it!" he yelped, clutching the top of his head.

He looked around for the child he had heard, but saw nothing.

"Hello, who's there?" he shouted, but the only reply came from a work colleague outside.

"You say something, Paul?" his manager yelled from the seat of his forklift.

"No, it's all right!" Paul shouted back, and he carried on taking boxes from a pallet in the aisle and putting them onto another pallet under the racking.

He was leaning towards the back of the pallet when he saw the pale face of a boy, about eight years old, staring at him through the racks from the aisle behind.

"Oi, you can't be in here!" Paul yelled at the kid, fearing for his safety in a dangerous warehouse. "Go back onto the shop floor!"

The child giggled and ran off, and Paul jogged around to the other aisle to find him, but when he got there the boy was nowhere to be seen and all was still.

Paul shook his head. "I blame the parents," he muttered to himself, not knowing the irony that he himself would have been this boy's father and responsible for his behaviour.

As he turned to go back to his racking away, he saw the malevolent brat standing at the end of the aisle. The boy waved at him and ran further into the warehouse.

"Bloody idiot," Paul whispered, then he shouted, "Stop messing around; it's not safe for you in here!"

Paul ran to the top end of the aisle where the urchin had been standing and looked around. He then heard the boy's giggle coming from the area where he had previously been racking away, so he ran to where the laugh had come from, but as he went he saw the boy dart across the end of the aisle, heading deeper into the warehouse.

Again Paul yelled, "Come here, you brat!" But the child was lost in the racking.

The forklift drivers were unaware of Paul's situation and they carried on unloading the lorry outside and bringing the delivery into the warehouse before dropping the pallets in the delivery area, which was a large square between the racking and the yard outside, kept clear for any incoming deliveries.

Paul continued to run up and down in between the racking, hoping to catch the menace, but each time he did, the boy was always just out of reach at the end of the aisle before running away again.

Paul suddenly stopped and stood still, listening for any noise, and sensed that there was an eerie and evil feeling around the warehouse as the atmosphere seemed to be closing in all around him.

At first all he could hear was the rumble of the forklift trucks, but then a shuffling noise came from halfway down an aisle. This time Paul didn't run; he quietly walked down the aisle, hoping to catch the infant.

He slowly paced through the racking, and as he walked past a pallet he didn't see the boy sitting cross-legged on it with an evil grin on his face. As Paul passed, the boy stood up and walked behind him and then patted

Paul on his shoulder. This made Paul jump and he let out a quiet yelp of surprise, and as he turned around he saw the child running back down the aisle, laughing.

"Now I've got you," Paul uttered to himself as he ran after him.

He saw the boy run through the racking and out into the delivery area, and with a smile said, "Ha – nowhere to run now."

Paul ran as fast as he could through the last of the racking and out into the delivery area, but as he sprinted forward a forklift truck was coming the other way, heading straight for him. The driver pressed down hard on the horn, letting out a loud shrill that shot through the air, but Paul was running too fast and he couldn't stop in time.

The driver shouted, "Paul!" but the sickening impact could not be stopped and Paul ran straight into the head-height forks. The truck screeched to a halt, but it was too late; Paul's head rammed into one of the forks and he was instantly decapitated. With a horrible cracking sound, his face was partially crushed by the force of the impact. His nose and eyes were pushed deep into his skull and his head was sent spinning through the air, back into the racking of the warehouse.

Paul's body remained upright, and a fountain of blood was gushing from the hole in his neck. The body, its nerves still active, quivered and trembled from the violent trauma it had just experienced, and the crimson liquid shot all around the delivery area, covering the boxes, pallets and labourers.

The workers stood there with their hands on their faces, not believing what had just happened. Then Paul's body collapsed, chest down on the ground with blood still gushing from the neck. It shot out towards the men, forming a slippery red path which made them slide to the floor.

As they all writhed and splashed about, screaming in the scarlet puddle of filth which covered their clothes and faces, they didn't see the laughing, diabolical boy walk back into the racking. He followed a thin red trail on the floor and found Paul's severed head with its still-open eyes staring out from the cavity in the skull which used to be Paul's face, sitting on a box in the aisle. His blood was dripping down and splashing onto the pallet and floor below. The horrid child then took out a King of Clubs card from his pocket and placed it over the eyes of his tragic victim, and it seemed to fit perfectly in the hole in the skull left behind by the crushing impact of the forklift truck. This was yet another victory for the Entertainer and his loathsome offspring.

THE MUSEUM

With the news of Paul's horrid death, Steve had got his men together to try and find the deceased's past girlfriends over the last twenty years in the hope of beating the Entertainer to his next victim.

He was at the police station, frantically organising his men. He pointed at an officer. "You go and find that Sharon Humber woman; we've got her address and she dated Paul about fifteen years ago."

The officer seemed unconcerned. "Really it's a long time ago; is it really necessary sir?

Steve glared at him. "Yes, it is. If we can save at least one of his past lovers, then we will. We've no idea how far back this all goes or which lover it is. We know it'll be one of his exes as the King of Clubs was found at the scene, so until we've got something more to go on, we'll do whatever we can."

Steve then walked up close to the officer and firmly said, "Sharon Humber."

The officer nodded and left the room to start his

investigations, and as he walked through the door, Josh came in.

"Any news yet, Steve?" he asked in the hope that things were moving on.

Steve pointed to the desk and they both sat down. He shuffled with some papers and then gave Josh an update.

"We know that Paul has been married for the last twelve years, so we're going back over the eight prior to that. His wife has given us some names and we've already got three previous girlfriends in protective custody. One of the others died about five years ago, leaving only two still to find."

Josh breathed a huge sigh of relief. "Well, at least we may have saved someone this time. What about the outstanding ones?"

Steve picked out some pictures from the papers on the desk. "Here they are." He examined the information on the sheets. "They are Sharon Humber and Tiffany Taylor. Someone is already on his way to Sharon and she has been contacted and told to stay indoors, and then there's Tiffany, thirty-four years old and last known to be living in Lincoln. We've already got people on their way to her, so hopefully we'll be in time."

Just then a policewoman came darting into the room and walked straight up to Steve.

"We've got a problem, sir: Tiffany wasn't at home. She's visiting relatives in either London or Edinburgh, and the neighbours can't confirm which it is."

"Damn!" Steve shouted as his fist came down hard

onto the desk. "It's never easy, is it?" Steve seemed to be defeated.

The room became silent and tense. None of the officers knew what to do or say; they were waiting for some inspiration from their boss. Josh looked at Steve and gave him some much-needed advice.

"Steve, find out where in London or Edinburgh she's gone and contact the police in those areas and tell them to find Tiffany. Tell them it's connected with the murders you're investigating and they'll do their best; it's all we can do"

Everyone in the room was watching Steve and waiting to see what would happen next. It was clear that he was feeling guilty and personally responsible for the deaths, and that he was under great strain and not really thinking clearly.

He let out a large breath and composed himself. "Yes Josh, you're right."

Turning to the sergeant, Steve ordered, "Contact the police in the areas where Tiffany might be and get her found but knowing our luck though she'll be the next victim before we can get to her."

The sergeant left the room and Josh glanced at Steve. "Let's hope we get to her in time."

***

While all of this was going on, Tiffany was walking around a very large museum in London and was oblivious to the threat facing her. She was enjoying the exhibits, and her favourite was the Egyptian section. She was looking closely at a Tutankhamen-style death mask which sat in a glass case on a decorated plinth.

She was reading the inscription about the mask's owner when she caught a glimpse of a young boy peering at her from the other side of the glass box. Tiffany smiled at him, but the boy just glared at her, which sent an icy chill down her spine. She looked away and slowly walked towards the wall to examine another exhibit. Again it was in a glass case on a plinth, and this time the exhibit was a mummified cat.

Tiffany's face contorted. "That's horrible," she whispered to herself, and she was just about to leave the display when she saw the same boy's face looking at her from the other side of the glass, just like before.

She shook her head at the boy and said to him with a smile, "You can't scare me."

She thought that the brat was trying to make her jump or something, but suddenly the smile dropped from her face and was replaced with a look of fright. She realised that the display case was actually sitting up against the wall and there was no room for anyone to get behind it. How could the boy be looking at her from the other side of the display?

Tiffany then sighed with relief and thought that the youngster must be standing behind her and she was actually looking at his reflection. She turned around to confront the urchin.

"You won't..." Her words suddenly stopped; there was no young boy standing behind her.

Tiffany quickly turned around and looked back into the display case, and her body became rigid with terror. The boy's face was still looking at her from the other side of the glass. She spun back around and looked all around the room; she was totally alone.

Suddenly, from behind an exhibit on the other side of the room, the troublesome brat ran out and laughed at Tiffany. This made her jump, but she was glad that she had actually seen the boy and wasn't going insane. She noticed that he was a bit scruffy, dishevelled and painfully thin. She felt a bit sorry for the lad, but this didn't last long as the boy suddenly jumped on top of a long glass display case and started to jump up and down on it.

With shock in her voice, Tiffany shouted, "Stop that, you idiot – you'll fall through the glass!" But the sinister nestling carried on leaping about.

Fearing for the boy as she didn't really want to get him into trouble, Tiffany walked towards him, and not wanting to draw attention from any of the museum's workers, she quietly said, "You'll set the alarms off; go on, get down from there."

This seemed to work as the boy jumped back down to the floor and stared at Tiffany. He then ran past her and went to the display containing the mummified cat. The brat grabbed the glass case and started to shake it.

Tiffany's face had a look of shock on it as she exclaimed, "Oh no you don't"

She looked around the room, and apart from the wicked minor she was still alone. She firmly paced towards him.

"Stop it now – if someone comes in they will think you're with me."

But the mischievous boy just shook the glass case harder, which made the cat mummy fall about inside.

A horrified Tiffany yelled, "Stop it now – the alarms will go off!"

She made a grab for the fiendish nipper, but he dodged her attempt and ran to the main display containing the death mask she had examined before. He gave an evil laugh as he gripped the display case and leered at Tiffany. Her eyes widened in anticipation of what would happen next.

"Get off the glass!" she said with a raised voice, "Enough now – just go away!"

But the Entertainer's evil offspring would not be stopped. He shook the case unnaturally fast and violently, which dislodged the mask from its stand. An alarm immediately rang out through the entire museum as the boy pushed the case to the floor, shattering it into hundreds of razor-sharp pieces. Workers and security guards could be heard shouting at the visitors to leave the building and gather in the car park, and panic surrounded the museum.

"Now look at what you've done!" Tiffany yelled at the child. "This is your fault!"

The boy just smiled at her, and then he faded away, leaving a shocked Tiffany totally alone in the room.

She looked at the damage left behind and muttered to herself, "I'm not getting blamed for all of this."

She turned to leave and ran straight into the arms of a security guard. There was an awkward pause before the guard said, "Go – get out of the museum and wait in the car park."

Tiffany nodded as the guard continued, "You'll be searched outside, but hurry as the security doors will come down."

Tiffany ran down a long passageway, and as she didn't really know the museum she was frantically looking for the exit signs. She stopped and looked around and saw the evil young boy standing at the end of a corridor. She pointed at him and yelled, "You – wait there!" But he just smiled at her and ran around the corner.

Tiffany ran after him, and as she did, a heavy, thick glass security door came sliding down from the ceiling, sealing off the corridor behind her. She ran and turned the corner to find herself in another corridor with the devilish brat at the far end. The boy laughed at her, and as before ran off around the corner at the end of the passageway.

"You ain't getting away!" she shouted at him, and she sprinted off to catch him. Again, a thick, heavy glass security door came sliding down from the ceiling behind her, sealing the passageway.

As Tiffany was sprinting as fast as she could, she quickly reached the end of the corridor, and as she turned the corner she saw that the boy had fallen and hurt his ankle. He was about halfway down the passageway in a heap on the floor, clutching his foot in pain. It was twisted around, facing the opposite direction. It was a horrible sight and the foot was obviously badly broken, but at least she knew there was now no escape for the brat.

"Now I've got you."

She slowly walked towards him, but then the brat stood up. This made Tiffany stop in her tracks; how could he stand with a broken and twisted foot? The youngster smiled at her and grabbed his injured foot. He then did something that made Tiffany sick in her own mouth: he started to twist it back into its correct position and the awful cracking and grinding of bone was heard as he put his foot back into its proper position. A piece of sharp bone suddenly burst out through his skin, which made Tiffany heave and she was nearly sick on the spot. The demonic child shrugged his shoulders and violently pushed the protruding bone back into his ankle. He then shook his mended leg, which now moved perfectly, and stood correctly on both feet glaring at Tiffany.

This was the moment that Tiffany realised that the boy was unnatural, and that she was in danger. She was rigid with fright, but she knew that she had to find the strength from somewhere to make her escape.

With a deep breath, she was ready to run, but it was too late. Before she could move, a heavy glass security door slammed down from the ceiling, slicing through her body from the top of her head to the very soles of her feet.

For a sickening moment she was stuck to the glass door with the front of her body on one side and the back on the other. The door had cut her in half vertically, slicing through every organ, piece of flesh, sinew and bone in its path. Even though she had died instantly, her eyes were open in horror, still staring at the diabolical boy, who still had an evil grin on his pale face.

The devilish child walked towards Tiffany, who was still pinned to both sides of the glass by her own body parts and sticky goo. Her blood began to seep out and run down the glass, which weakened the bond and the back half of her body peeled away from the glass like old wallpaper and fell to the ground in a horrid, folded heap of mess. The bond sticking her front half to the barrier began to lose its integrity and slowly, with an ear-piercing screech, slid down to the floor with knees bending, leaving a sickly trail of organs and blood smeared down the glass.

The horrid boy walked over to the bloody mess and placed the King of Clubs playing card on Tiffany's face, which was looking upwards from the top of the folded pile with her cold, dead eyes still staring out into nothing.

He then stood back and faded away, leaving the carnage behind to be found by someone else.

THE THIRTEENTH

Later on that day the news of Tiffany's horrible demise had reached Steve and Josh at the police station. They were too late to save her, but they knew that there would only be one more death to make up the thirteen.

"It's getting a bit late now," a defeated Steve muttered to Josh. "There's not a lot more we can do today unless our investigation comes up with something else but this is a weird one and The Entertainer or whoever it is always seems one step ahead of us."

Josh nodded in agreement. "All right, I'll see you tomorrow."

He left the station and bumped into Maggie. He sighed and shook his tired head. "Come on, Mags, let's go for a walk."

Maggie knew the investigation wasn't going too well and could see that Josh was a bit down so she took him by the hand. "OK, let's go along the beach."

It was late in the evening and turning a bit darker, and the two of them slowly walked hand in hand along the beach. They were talking and trying to figure out why the Entertainer had promised an odd number of deaths, as if the victims were the potential parents of the ghost children, surely there should be two deaths for each couple?

Then Maggie remembered her dream about Midway and the Entertainer and said, "It all started when the elder's daughter was killed by the Entertainer's skipping device."

Josh agreed. "Yes, but we still don't know exactly what it all means."

They reached a trail through the sand dunes which led to the chalet park where Maggie lived. They hugged and she started to walk alone down the trail. Looking back, she said, "See you tomorrow, Josh. Things may be clearer in the morning."

Josh waved her goodbye and walked back along the beach to go home, soothed by the gentle sounds of the waves flowing onto the sand and the soft breeze brushing his face.

***

Maggie soon got home to her chalet and she went straight into the bedroom, fell down onto the bed and was soon in a deep sleep. Once again, she began to dream about Midway, and again she found herself witnessing the lynch mob massing, ready to kill Bartholomew Smith and his family.

"Mr Hannah, what shall we do first?" one of the men asked his leader.

The elder thought for a second and then loudly announced, "We'll burn the house first. Burn it all!"

The mob shouted and cheered as they lit torches from a near-by fire and walked towards the home of the Entertainer and his family.

Maggie felt that she was again the twelve-year-old girl who lived in the village, and she could actually feel the violence and hatred of the mob. Once again the house was torched, killing the Entertainer's family. Then came the Entertainer's screams from his circus tent and just like before, the mob went to the marquee and burnt it to the ground, killing the vengeful Entertainer.

The crowd cheered and congratulated the elder for leading the mob and shouts of "Well done, Mr Hannah well done." were heard by all involved.

Maggie then suddenly awoke and sat bolt upright on her bed. "Elder Hannah," she whispered. "Why does that name trouble me?"

She got up and went into the kitchen to make herself a late-night coffee, still puzzled and affected by her dream. Still thinking about the importance of the name, she kept saying to herself, "Hannah, Hannah – where have I heard that name before?"

The kettle boiled and she picked it up to pour the hot water into her mug, but she didn't pour it out. Maggie slammed the kettle back down.

"Oh no, *Hannah*" She had just remembered where she saw the name before; it was on a family coat of arms in Josh's house.

She picked up her phone and called him, but there was no answer so she left a message.

"It's Maggie, the name Hannah is important – it was

elder Hannah who led the lynch mob and I saw the same name on the coat of arms in your house. I'm on my way to find you now; please phone me when you get this message."

She picked up her coat and ran out of the chalet as fast as she could; she knew that she was on to something and that Josh may be in danger. She got into her car and drove away to find her friend.

Maggie drove out of the chalet park gates and down to the end of the short road leading to the main seafront road. She turned right and headed into the town, driving as fast but as safely as she could with her head spinning with thoughts of Josh or his family being in danger. Suddenly a feeling of dread fell over her and she glanced out of her side window and was terrified at what she saw.

Standing in a small field at the side of the road was a poor-looking, dishevelled young girl with deathly pale grey skin. The girl was about eleven years old and had shoulder-length dirty blonde hair, and her cold, dead eyes just looked at Maggie with a fixed, evil stare. She raised a bony finger and pointed at Maggie as she sped past. Maggie watched the girl as she passed and lost her concentration for a split second, but that was all that was needed for the Entertainer to appear in the road ahead.

When Maggie looked forward again, she saw Bartholomew Smith leaning on his cane in the road in front of her. She slammed down hard on the brakes, but she didn't have time to stop and swerved violently to the left and smashed into a wall.

The front of her car was a crumpled mess and Maggie had blood running down her face from the impact with the steering wheel, but she was alive. She regained a degree of composure and looked out of the window to see Bartholomew Smith peering straight at her with an evil grin on his face.

"I have been watching you, Maggie," he said. "You are close to understanding my reasons and actions, but not close enough."

Maggie was scared, but she summoned the strength to speak. "I know one thing," she replied with a cough. "We're on to you, and you will fail."

This made the Entertainer angry, and he slammed his cane down onto the roof of the car, which made Maggie jump with fright.

"I never fail!" he bellowed, getting closer to Maggie's bloodied face. "I always complete what I set out to do perfectly."

Maggie laughed. "You've made a mistake this time, though; you can't even add up properly."

Bartholomew was puzzled and upset by this, so quizzed Maggie, "What do you mean?"

"Thirteen!" Maggie shouted in his face. "There are to be thirteen deaths. If you are killing couples, there would be an even number."

Bartholomew stood back a little. "Ah, thirteen," he cackled. "You're wrong, my dear; thirteen is the correct number. Chris Andrews died about five years ago, so I can't kill him as death has already taken him, but I can still kill his ex-girlfriend Rosie, can't I?"

Maggie then realised who the last victim would be: it was Rosie, Josh's wife.

The Entertainer raised his cane high into the air and was just about to bring it down onto a weakened and vulnerable Maggie when a shout was heard a short distance away. It was a man who had seen Maggie's car crash into the wall, and he was running to help her.

Bartholomew Smith slowly lowered his cane. "You're lucky this time," the disappointed Entertainer mumbled, "but I'll be back for you."

He then doffed his top hat at Maggie and faded away just as she fainted.

***

Josh was in a cafe in one of the arcades, finishing off a hot chocolate, when the waitress walked over to him.

"We're closing now, Josh," she said, sensing he had a lot on his mind. "Go home."

Josh looked up at her and smiled. "OK, see you again."

He left the arcade and headed to his car, taking his phone from his pocket as he walked. He turned it back on and put it to his ear. His jaw dropped as he heard Maggie's message about the name Hannah, and he jogged to his car, hoping to go to Maggie's chalet. As he got nearer he saw Steve leaning on the bonnet, and he looked a bit troubled.

"Josh, where have you been? I've been phoning you all night but your phone's been off."

"I just needed some quiet time, Steve," Josh replied. "What do you want?"

Steve sighed. "There's been an accident. Maggie's hurt and the doc's got her at the surgery as she needed treatment straight away. An ambulance has already been called and should get here soon."

"My God, what happened?" a worried Josh asked. "How is she?"

Steve made a calming gesture with his hands. "Don't worry, she should be fine; she had a crash while driving to find you and she seemed in a panic – something about the name Hannah."

Josh gave Steve a troubled look and uttered, "Hannah was Rosie's maiden name and I don't know where she is. She's not been answering her phone all day and I think she may be the next death on our hands."

"OK, I'll get my men to look for her and you go to Maggie; she may be able to help," Steve suggested. Josh agreed and drove to the surgery to see Maggie.

***

He arrived at the doctor's surgery and it looked a bit spooky in the darkness of the night, as some of the lights were on but it was well past closing time. He got out of his car and was greeted by Dr Freestone.

"Ah, Josh, we've been expecting you," he said as they shook hands. "She's a bit sore but she'll be all right with a bit of rest."

"Thanks, Doc, and thanks for opening the surgery to treat her," a relieved Josh replied.

"Not a problem, Josh. I've just got to go home to get something, though; I'll be gone about ten minutes. Just go in."

The doctor left and Josh went into the surgery and entered the treatment room where he saw Maggie on the bed with a bandage around her head.

She opened her eyes, and in a panic said, "Josh, quick – what does the name Hannah mean to you?"

Josh sat down on a chair beside the bed. "Hannah was Rosie's maiden name. Is she in danger?" he said while trying to phone Rosie yet again.

Maggie sat up, and with a worried look on her face replied, "I'm not sure; she may be. Did she ever go out with a Chris Andrews?"

Josh became more nervous and concerned for his wife as he held his mobile to his ear calling Rosie but she still failed to answer her phone. "Yes, they went out together years ago when she was about twenty. It was Chris who actually introduced Rosie to me, but he died about five years ago. Why?"

"Oh, Josh, I'm so sorry," Maggie said with a slight tremble in her voice, "That confirms that Rosie will be the Entertainer's last victim."

Suddenly it dawned on Josh, and he shuddered. "That's why there are an odd number of deaths. I've got to find Rosie"

Maggie nodded. "I bet Rosie's missing, isn't she?"

Josh stood up and looked out of the window into the darkness outside. After a few seconds he turned and looked at Maggie. "I don't know where she is; she's not answered her phone all day and Steve and the police are already looking for her."

"Go and see Bill Grimes; he's your last hope,"

suggested a very worried Maggie. "He might have some ideas."

Josh nodded, "Good call, Maggie." He kissed her on the cheek. "I'll go now; you just rest and get stronger and I'll see you in the morning."

Josh ran out of the door as Maggie shouted, "Good luck – see you tomorrow!"

***

Josh raced down the road and up the dirt path to the house of old Mr Grimes and jumped out of his car. He ran to the door and banged loudly on it.

"Mr Grimes" His shouts rang out in the night. "Mr Grimes, it's urgent!"

The front door flew open and Mr Grimes stood there with a shotgun raised and pointed at Josh. The hermit then recognised him and lowered his gun.

"Josh, what's wrong?"

Josh struggled for breath as he said, "Maggie's been hurt and my wife is in danger."

Mr Grimes ushered Josh inside and they stood in the hallway.

"As you already know my name is Bill, Mr Grimes' seems too formal my friend. How can I help?"

Josh was a little calmer now, and appealed to Bill. "My wife Rosie is missing, I think the Entertainer might have her and I need ideas as to where she may be."

Bill nodded. "After you left the other day, I did some research of my own. I think the Entertainer needs a certain physical connection with our time to finish his work, and the only thing I can think of is the old abandoned house further up the coast on the very edge of the clifftop. It used to belong to his family."

Josh's eyes widened "Do you mean Waterloo Manor, that old run-down mansion that's nearly falling into the sea?"

Mr Grimes gave a broad smile. "That's exactly where I mean, and if you hurry you just might be in time."

Without any delay, Josh thanked Bill and rushed out of the house. He got into his car and drove to Waterloo Manor in the hope of saving his beloved Rosie.

***

Back at the doctor's surgery, Maggie was sitting up and having a sip of water.

"Where's that bloody doctor gone? He's been ages," she whispered to herself.

Then she heard a noise coming from outside her room, so she shouted, "Doc, is that you?"

The door opened and Bartholomew Smith himself walked in. Behind him, the same pale-skinned young girl from earlier stayed in the doorway.

"I told you I'd be back for you, didn't I?"

Maggie was rigid with fright, and she couldn't even speak.

The Entertainer quickly walked over to the horrified woman and spoke the last words that Maggie would ever hear. "You have caused me trouble for the last time."

He pulled out the handle of his cane to reveal a secret sword hidden inside. Without any hesitation at all he swung the blade through the air and sliced Maggie's head clean off.

The head flew from her sitting body and landed on the floor with her open eyes staring up at him; open eyes when dead seemed to be a common trait and liked in the killings. Blood spurted up out of her neck and splattered on the ceiling above before cascading back down like a deep red waterfall all over Maggie's body and bed. Scarlet blood oozed out from under her decapitated head and seeped all over the floor, turning the colour of the carpet from beige to a sickly shade of claret.

The Entertainer removed a Joker playing card from his sleeve and placed it on Maggie's chest, laughed and turned to the door, where the young girl was still standing. He smiled and walked up to her.

"Come, my child," he said lovingly as he put his arm around her. "Let us go and complete our revenge."

WATERLOO

Josh had now reached the deserted mansion on the clifftop where he hoped he would find his wife. It was a spooky old place and bats were flying around the area. Overgrown, thorn-covered bushes were everywhere, and the house hadn't been lived in or taken care of for years. He didn't know that the Entertainer was already inside, planning Rosie's demise. Josh walked up the short, dusty pathway to the front door and tried the handle, but the door was locked. He looked around on the ground and saw a large rock, which he picked up and, without a second's thought, threw through the window, shattering the glass.

***

The smash was heard in a room upstairs where the Entertainer was preparing for Rosie's death. She was securely strapped to a chair in front of a large window. The faint glow of the night's first glimpse of moonlight forced its way through the dirt and grime stuck to the glass. There was a sheer, deadly drop down onto the cliffs below it.

Rosie's feet were tied to the chair's legs and her hands and arms tightly fixed to its arms. There was even a leather strap around her waist, securing her to the back of the chair. She tried to scream, but her voice was muffled by the thick strip of tape the Entertainer had placed firmly over her mouth. Tears of fright rolled down her cheeks and her mouth was struggling to open and close behind the tape, trying to force out sounds to attract anyone's attention who she hoped would be able to save her, but she was only producing faint noises. There was a noose tied around her neck, and the other end of the rope led out of a small pane of glass in the window behind and was tied to a wooden frame protruding outside from above.

The Entertainer looked at the terrified woman. "Ah, it sounds like your beloved husband has arrived."

The young, wicked girl who had been with the Entertainer on the road and at the doctor's surgery walked over to Rosie and tightened the noose around her slender neck, which forced a muffled yelp from Rosie's mouth. The girl then spoke words that horrified the securely fastened woman.

"There we go, Mother; we don't want it to fall off, do we?"

Rosie's stunned eyes opened wide and she slowly shook her head. The loathsome creature then grabbed her by the hair and peered deeply into her eyes.

"Take a good, hard look, Rosie," the Entertainer said with an evil smile. "See what you can see."

Rosie stared into the girl's dead, black eyes and the tears rolled down her face faster than before as she seemed to recognise something about the sinister nestling, some kind of vague, long-gone connection. An understanding began to dawn on Rosie, but she didn't know exactly what it meant. Then the evil child let Rosie's head go and stepped back.

"OK, let's get started, shall we?" Bartholomew said with a cackle. "This is going to be a good one."

A very large and heavy sledgehammer was fixed to a pivot on the ceiling by its handle, which made it swing like a crude sword of Damocles, waiting to harm its victim below. However, Bartholomew Smith didn't hang the hammer directly above Rosie. A length of strong reinforced string was also tied near to the head of the hammer which threaded through a brass ring that was also fixed to the ceiling, and when this string was pulled it forced the heavy hammer up to the ceiling, where it stayed in a dangerous horizontal position.

Smith walked over to the door of the room with the end of this string in his hand. He opened the door, put the string against the inner door frame, and carefully closed the door, trapping the string as he did so. Whoever opened the door would release the hammer and send it swooping down into Rosie's chest, and we all know who that person would be.

Bartholomew Smith then walked back into the centre of the room, raised his bony finger and pointed to the door. "Go on, my child, go and help Josh to find us."

Rosie started to move around on the chair in panic,

and again muffled screams came from her tightly taped mouth as the ghastly young girl went over to the door where she silently and somewhat gracefully walked right through it without opening it.

***

Downstairs, Josh was quietly walking from room to room, looking for his wife. He tried the handles of various doors but most of them were locked and had been for quite a few years, and the ones that opened only revealed empty and dusty rooms.

Suddenly he had the horrible feeling that he was being watched. He slowly turned around and was stunned at what he saw. The dishevelled, fiendish young girl was standing in the middle of the large hallway, and immediately he knew she was one of the Entertainer's evil offspring.

Josh pointed at her. "You stay right there and don't move!" he shouted. "Where's my wife?"

The girl laughed and slowly walked to the bottom of the stairs, where she stood, ready to run up them to lure Josh to the room where his beloved Rosie was.

Josh sensed she was ready to run and said, "Oh no you don't."

The demonic child smiled and ran up the stairs, with Josh running as fast as he could in pursuit. As he reached the top of the stairway, he turned and found himself looking down a long landing with many doors leading off it. But where did the child go? Josh turned around and looked the other way, but there was no sign of her so he turned back to the long corridor. This time, the ghostly girl was standing outside the room where the Entertainer and Rosie were waiting.

"Don't you move" Josh said as he pointed at her, but she just walked straight through the door and disappeared from sight.

Josh walked slowly down the passageway and stood outside the door. He grabbed the handle, but hesitated for a few seconds as he sensed something was wrong. He removed his hand from the handle and stood back, wondering if he should go in or not. He wanted to enter the room, but something told him not to.

***

Inside the room, Bartholomew Smith knew he had to do something, so he walked up to Rosie and whispered, "It seems he needs a little encouragement."

He put his hand up to her mouth and ripped off the tape which had been gagging her.

Instinctively she screamed, "Josh!"

But that was the worst thing she could've done.

***

Josh heard Rosie's scream, and as fast as he could he grabbed the door handle, turned it, and ran into the room.

As soon as the door was flung open, it released the string securing the hammer and sent the heavy load swinging downwards towards Rosie. For the split second before the hammer hit its target, Josh's eyes and Rosie's met across the room. They both knew what was about to happen, but it was too late. With Rosie still tied to the chair, the sledgehammer swooped and smashed into her chest splitting her skin open as it crushed her ribs. A sickening crack was heard as her ribcage pressed inwards, puncturing her lungs and heart, sending thin sprays of flesh and blood jetting into the room and doing untold internal damage.

The helpless woman, still fixed to the chair, was lifted off the floor by the force of the hammer blow, and the Entertainer and the evil girl laughed loudly just before Rosie was sent crashing out of the window behind her. She dropped down the cliff face below, and the rope snapped her neck as it tightened about halfway down. Josh had killed his own wife just by opening the door.

Rosie dangled down the cliff face, turning slightly in the night's breeze. The vile young girl walked up to the shocked Josh and handed him a King of Clubs playing card.

"You'll need this," she muttered.

Josh looked down at the card and came to his senses. He ran to the window and screamed, "Rosie, Rosie, no!" but he knew she was gone.

He grabbed the rope and started to pull Rosie up as Bartholomew said to the girl, "Come, let us gather our souls – it's over now."

Bartholomew and the wretched child walked out of the room as Josh, with adrenaline fuelled strength somehow pulled Rosie up and back through the window.

The heavy chair, still bound to her body, banged onto the floor. He untied his dead wife and cried as he hugged her.

"I'm so sorry, Rosie," he sobbed, "I didn't know."

Eventually Josh composed himself and stood up, leaving Rosie on the floor.

"I'll come back for you, I promise," he whispered. He knew he had to follow the Entertainer.

He tore up the card in his hands and left the room to think about what Smith had just said.

"Gather the souls," he muttered to himself. "Now, where would an entertainer go to gather his souls?"

Then it dawned on him and he blurted out, "The fairground!"

Josh ran to his car and drove to the funfair where he hoped to somehow stop the Entertainer, but he hadn't a clue what he would do.

***

He drove as fast as he could back into Mablethorpe and along the coast road towards the fairground. As he got nearer he could see some faint lights in the distance near the gates of the funfair. His eyes adjusted as he approached and he was horrified to realise that the lights were the ghostly, grey forms of the Entertainer's victims, and they were all slowly disappearing up the few steps at the entrance of the fair and through its locked gates.

Josh then saw the sad, dull light of Rosie and she was the last in the ghostly line, so he drove faster and then slammed his brakes on and skidded as he reached the fair.

He got out of his car and sprinted to the steps, calling out to Rosie as he started to run up them. He stretched out his arm in the hope of actually grabbing her, but he stumbled and fell to the ground.

Composing himself, Josh quickly looked up to the top of the steps and saw that Rosie was just about to glide through the gates. He ran as fast as he could back up the steps and held out his hand, but it was too late; he missed Rosie by mere inches as she passed effortlessly through the shut metal gates.

Josh crashed into the gates and stretched out his arm through the bars, but it was all in vain – Rosie was out of reach.

Tears ran down his face as the devastated man yelled, "Rosie!"

The shout made Rosie glance back towards her husband, and there was some sad recognition but it didn't last long and she turned and walked further into the funfair, where she sat in a dodgem car.

Wiping away his tears, Josh saw that all of the ghostly victims were going to various rides and stalls – some went to the waltzers, some to the ghost train, and some to a shooting range. One even went to the hook-a-duck stall and sat down on top of the floating plastic ducks.

He then saw Bartholomew Smith standing near the centre of the fairground. Josh saw everything quite clearly as the fairground wasn't that big and the way the rides and stalls were set out made the fair easy to see from one end to the other. The Entertainer then raised his cane high into the air and all of his demonic, vile children began to emerge from their hiding places behind different stalls and rides and gather around their master.

A victorious smile beamed all over his face as he spoke to his hateful descendants.

"Go on, my children," he bellowed; the evil grin still on his face. "Go and have your last play!"

With an eerie sense of magic, all of the fair's rides and attractions started up and their music began to play. This was obviously the signal for the children to choose what rides they would go on and who to torture as they then began to make their way to their preferred victims.

One urchin went to the waltzers, and as the ride spun round the child spun the seat with the ghostly victim inside, which made the victim bang from side to side in the carriage. Another child was shooting pellets on the rifle range, and as they passed through the head of another victim standing in front of the targets, the doomed man let out screams of pain. Three of the poor wretches were in one of the seats of the ghost train, and a fiendish nestling was standing behind them as they disappeared into the ride. Painful wails and shrieks were heard outside; there was no telling how they were being tortured. The man sitting in the hook-a-duck stall was being beaten by two of the ghostly children with the hooks, and this scene was being played out all over the fairground in various different ways. Each child was inflicting injury upon the innocent sufferers, causing them distress and pain in their undead state.

Josh looked towards the dodgem cars where he saw Rosie and other casualties of the Entertainer being rammed hard by malicious brats who were laughing as they drove into their targets. Rosie was being tossed from side to side in her seat, and her head shook violently to and fro. Josh saw one of the victims being sliced in half on the mini roller coaster towards the rear of the fair; even in death there was no rest from Entertainer and his evil children's torture.

Josh looked back at Rosie and the tears began to fall down his cheeks once again.

Suddenly, the Entertainer stared at him and shouted out into the night, "I am Bartholomew Smith, the Entertainer, and I finally have my revenge!"

He then walked a little closer to the locked gates where Josh was kneeling and looking longingly through the bars at Rosie. Bartholomew gracefully swung his cane as he bowed down low, and as he rose back up, he spoke some final words to Josh.

"Who will be the next to enjoy all the fun of the scare?"

Bartholomew chuckled loudly as he turned and walked back to the centre of the fair, where he disappeared into a strange mist. The victims' tortured screams of agony and the children's evil laughter faded away and echoed in the emptiness of the ungodly night sky as they also vanished, leaving the fairground totally still. A revolting smell filled the air and everything was in complete darkness, and all that was left in the putrid atmosphere was an eerie silence.

ABOUT THE AUTHOR

Rooster was born and raised in the Midlands, where he works in the industrial sector. He likes horror, comedy, the coast, rock music and live concerts.

This is his debut novel and the first of a trilogy.

ACKNOWLEDGEMENTS

I am eternally grateful for the help and support from my wife Karen; my children Jenna, Adam and Stacie; my mum Barbara; my siblings Angie and Carl; and all of my family and close friends.

I must give a personal and special thank-you to my brother Carl for his direct input in getting this book published, and to my son Adam who said, "Just write a book, Dad"; so I did.

I love and thank you all…